PRAISE FOR

TROUBLEMAKER

"A **compelling story in a vivid setting** that has not been explored enough in books for young readers. Jordan is a genuine, flawed character so real you can't help rooting for him. Deep appreciation to authors John Cho and Sarah Suk for writing this **much-needed book**."
—**LINDA SUE PARK**,
Newbery Medal winner and *New York Times* bestselling author

"**An action-packed adventure** that will not only quicken your pulse but make you think deeply about friendship, family, and justice."
—**NICOLA YOON**,
#1 *New York Times* bestselling author of *The Sun Is Also a Star* and *Instructions for Dancing*

"**Fast-paced yet thoughtful and profound**, *Troublemaker* revisits the fires of the past to shine light and wisdom for a better future."
—**DAVID YOON**,
New York Times bestselling author of *Frankly in Love*

"A **heartfelt, insightful** book exploring the bond between father and son who deepen their relationship while navigating social justice, police bias, Korean American identity, and the trauma of the LA riots."
—**JEWELL PARKER RHODES**,
bestselling author of *Ghost Boys* and *Paradise on Fire*

TROUBLEMAKER

JOHN CHO

with SARAH SUK

LITTLE, BROWN AND COMPANY

New York Boston

Copyright © 2022 by John Cho

Cover art copyright © 2022 by Chris Danger. Cover design by Karina Granda. Cover copyright © 2022 by Hachette Book Group, Inc.

Hachette Book Group supports the right to free expression and the value of copyright. The purpose of copyright is to encourage writers and artists to produce the creative works that enrich our culture.

The scanning, uploading, and distribution of this book without permission is a theft of the author's intellectual property. If you would like permission to use material from the book (other than for review purposes), please contact permissions@hbgusa.com. Thank you for your support of the author's rights.

Little, Brown and Company
Hachette Book Group
1290 Avenue of the Americas, New York, NY 10104
Visit us at LBYR.com

First Edition: March 2022

Little, Brown and Company is a division of Hachette Book Group, Inc. The Little, Brown name and logo are trademarks of Hachette Book Group, Inc.

The publisher is not responsible for websites (or their content) that are not owned by the publisher.

Library of Congress Cataloging-in-Publication Data
Names: Cho, John, 1972– author. | Suk, Sarah, author.
Title: Troublemaker / John Cho with Sarah Suk.
Description: First edition. | New York ; Boston : Little, Brown and Company, 2022. | Audience: Ages 8–12. | Summary: On the first night of rioting in the wake of the Rodney King verdict, Jordan's father leaves to check on the family store, spurring twelve-year-old Jordan and his friends to embark on a dangerous journey through South Central and Koreatown to come to his aid, encountering the racism within their community as they go.
Identifiers: LCCN 2021029222 | ISBN 9780759554474 (hardcover) | ISBN 9780759554450 (ebook)
Subjects: CYAC: Family life—California—Los Angeles—Fiction. | Korean Americans—Fiction. | Rodney King Riots, Los Angeles, Calif., 1992—Fiction. | Race relations—Fiction. | Los Angeles (Calif.)—History—20th century—Fiction. | LCGFT: Novels.
Classification: LCC PZ7.1.C53117 Tr 2022 | DDC [Fic]—dc23
LC record available at https://lccn.loc.gov/2021029222

ISBNs: 978-0-7595-5447-4 (hardcover), 978-0-7595-5445-0 (ebook)

Printed in the United States of America

LSC-C

Printing 1, 2022

For my mother and father

CHAPTER ONE

April 29, 1992

I never knew a pair of shoes could scare me so much, but when I see Umma's and Appa's sneakers by the door when I walk in, I nearly jump right out of my skin. It's not that they're anything out of the ordinary. The shoes, I mean, with Appa's laces fraying at the ends and Umma's looking more gray than white like they did when she first bought them. What's weird is the fact that they're here at all. It's just a little after four PM on a Wednesday and Umma and Appa should both be at the store. Not at home.

I thought I'd have more time before I'd have to face them today.

Their voices are quiet, muffled, coming from the direction of the kitchen. I stand real still by the door, listening, but I can't hear what they're saying from here. I move carefully down the hall, gripping the straps of my backpack with both hands, praying in my head. *Don't see me. Don't see me.*

Just as I'm about to pass the kitchen, Umma looks right up at me.

"Oh, Jordan, you're home?" she says in Korean. She says it all casual like she's here every day when I get home from school, like I'm not the one who should be saying, "Oh, Umma, *you're* home?"

"Yeah," I say back in English. A nervous feeling starts to spread through my stomach. My prayer changes. *Don't ask me how school was. Don't make me lie to you.*

By some miracle, she doesn't. She just smiles and nods, turning back to Appa to carry on talking about whatever they were talking about, the air kind of tense and tight between them.

Huh. That's weird. Umma always asks how school was. It's pretty much her favorite question. Not to mention, I still don't know what they're both doing home so early.

I linger by the door, wondering whether I should ask or not. But the more questions I ask them, the more questions they might ask me. And I want to avoid that for as long as possible.

Not that Appa would ask me anything, though. This whole time, he hasn't even looked at me once. I don't know whether to be relieved or disappointed.

It's been this way between us for weeks, ever since our Big Fight. Things haven't been the same since then. It's like time split into a Before and After. Before: when I was just Jordan and he was just Appa, and I didn't think twice about being in the same room together. After: when we're not just Jordan and Appa anymore. We're Jordan Who Doesn't Know What to Say Around Appa, and Appa Who Basically Completely Ignores Jordan. He's been so cold to me lately. Ice cold.

Maybe he's waiting for me to say sorry first, but there's no way I'm going to do that.

Maybe this means we'll never talk again until the end of time. Maybe not even then.

I stare at the back of his head for a second longer and then I walk away.

Harabeoji's in the living room, watching TV and eating ojingeo off a plate. At least grandparents are dependable. Always where you think they'll be, sitting on the couch wearing a fishing vest with a hundred pockets even though you can't remember the last time you've ever actually seen them go fishing, a piece of dried squid between their teeth. At least, that's my grandpa. I don't really know about anyone else's grandparents.

"Hi, Harabeoji, I'm home," I say, dropping my backpack on the floor and sitting down next to it.

He grunts, not looking up from the TV. He's watching some sitcom I don't recognize—his favorites are usually *Full House* and *Home Improvement*—the light reflecting off his huge rectangular glasses. Harabeoji's not much of a talker, except when it comes to yelling at fictional characters on the screen. I don't even know if he knows what's going on. It's been nine years since we immigrated to Los Angeles from Korea all together and I'm still not sure how much English he understands.

He didn't want to come with us at first. To America, that is. He wanted to stay in Korea in the same house where he and my grandma had lived together for years, saying he wanted to die in the same room she did. But Appa said it would be the best thing for all of us, and that he wasn't going to leave his own father behind. He eventually convinced Harabeoji to pack up his life and get on the plane with us, though I remember Harabeoji being unhappy about it. At least he's found some joy in these American shows. I think he finds them funny.

I glance toward the kitchen and then back at Harabeoji, lowering my voice. "Can I tell you something?"

He grunts again without turning down the volume.

Here's the thing about my grandpa. We're not close exactly, but he's the one person in this family that I feel like I can really talk to, even if he doesn't totally get what I'm saying since I speak to him in English. Maybe that's the reason why I feel okay. Or maybe it's because he's too busy judging made-up people on television to judge me, and I know that whatever I tell him, he won't tell anyone else.

"I got suspended from school today."

At this, his eyebrows lift. I can't be sure if it's from what I said or from something on TV, but I keep going.

"I got sent to the principal's office again. For cheating on a Spanish quiz. Or I guess, getting caught cheating.

Again. Mr. Martins was so mad." I make a face, hearing his voice in my head. He always talks real slow like he's speaking through a mouth full of chewing gum. "He kept saying how he's seen me in his office more than any other sixth grader in the school and how he can't even count how many times I've been caught cheating now. And then you know what he says? He says I should try to be more like Sarah. Says that when *she* was in middle school, she was a model student. How could the Park siblings be this different? She probably makes your parents so proud. And you? Well, they'll be so disappointed in you, won't they?"

I scoff, but I can feel my shoulders slumping.

Mr. Martins doesn't need to tell me what a disappointment I am to my parents.

I already know that.

Appa told me so himself.

Harabeoji turns off the TV, startling me. He leans forward in his seat, his left hand on his knee. He's only got three fingers on that hand. He lost the pinky and ring finger during the Korean War. Umma says it's rude to stare, but it's hard not to when I'm sitting on the floor and basically eye level with it. I look at his face instead. He locks his eyes on mine, his mouth set in a grim line.

Uh-oh. Did I overestimate how safe my secrets are with him? My face flushes. Is he going to rat me out to Umma and Appa after all?

He holds out his empty plate with his right hand. "Get me more ojingeo," he says in Korean. "I ate it all."

Oh. Of course.

"Yes, Harabeoji."

I take the empty plate and head for the kitchen. But as I get closer, I can hear Umma and Appa talking, only it's not in those low voices I heard earlier. They're louder now, almost yelling. Are they fighting?

I stay in the hallway, listening. My Korean's not so great anymore, but I can understand more than I can speak, and I pick up every word.

"I think you're worrying too much about nothing," Appa says.

"You can never be too careful," Umma says back. She sounds exasperated, angry. "People are mad about what happened with Rodney King. Tell me you're not even a little bit worried that something bad might come out of that today."

"Of course they're mad. Who wouldn't be mad?" Now Appa's the one who sounds annoyed. "Doesn't mean that bad things are going to happen. There's no reason to think so. It will be fine."

"You heard what they said on Radio Korea. They said there may be protests so we should pay attention, stay alert—"

"And we did, didn't we? We closed the shop early and came home. That's enough. You're always thinking further ahead than you need to."

"How do you think I've carried us this far? I won't let this store fail like our last one. Someone has to think about this family!"

It's like she's sucker-punched him with her words. There's this long silence and I don't even realize it at first, but I'm holding my breath. I feel like if I let it out, the plate in my hands will crack, the air will explode, and Harabeoji will never get his squid because there's thunder and lightning standing between me and the kitchen.

Umma is the thunder. Maybe she's the lightning too.

"Fine," she finally says. "I'll go."

"Go where?"

"To board up the store."

Before Appa can reply or I can even take a step, Umma storms out of the kitchen. She doesn't see me. She's too focused, pushing the little wisps of hair falling from her stubby ponytail out of her eyes and reaching for the coat closet. She grabs the handle of the sliding mirrored door and pulls hard.

What happens next is everything shatters.

At first, I think I've dropped Harabeoji's plate, but when I look down, it's still in my hands. It wasn't me that broke. It was Umma.

The closet door's always been too flimsy, teetering on loose tracks, and Umma's pulled it open so hard it finally gave up and jumped the tracks. The whole mirrored door cracks and explodes into shards on the floor. She yells, jumps back, and then stands there, breathing heavy.

"What was that?" Harabeoji shouts from the living room.

"Everything's fine!" Umma shouts back, even though I think what she means is really the opposite.

Appa comes out of the kitchen and looks at Umma, standing there with that broken mirror all around her. Then he notices me.

Sometimes I forget how tall he is, but when he looks at me, he has to look way down the way I do when I look at ants on the sidewalk. He stares and I stare back, right at his bushy eyebrows and the permanent furrow in his brow like God stuck his thumb there for too long and left a dent. It's the first time we've really made eye contact since the Big Fight.

I'm bracing myself all over.

I think maybe he's going to say something.

And he does. But not to me.

He walks over to Umma and puts his hands on her shoulders. "I'll go board up the store," he says. "I'll call you when I'm there."

Then he reaches into the doorless coat closet and grabs his jacket, takes his car keys off the hook on the wall, puts on his shoes with the fraying laces, and leaves.

He doesn't look back once.

CHAPTER TWO

By the time Sarah comes home, the mirror's been all swept up and thrown away. You'd never know what happened. Except for the mirrorless door leaning against the hallway wall, obviously. But if Sarah notices, she doesn't say anything. Instead, she heads straight for the TV.

Sarah's a junior in high school and probably the busiest teenager in all of Glendale. Maybe even all of LA. She's always coming home late from some kind of after-school activity. It's no joke. She's part of every club, volunteers for every school event, and still somehow has time to hang out with her friends, driving around the city in the old beat-up

Hyundai Excel that Umma and Appa passed down to her for her sixteenth birthday.

She's one of those people that does everything right. Good manners, perfect grades, tons of friends. Adults love her. Me? I think she's a suck-up. Our parents even let her sleep over at her friends' houses. They never let me sleep over anywhere.

Umma, Harabeoji, and I are already gathered around the TV, eyes glued to the news. It's been a couple of hours since Appa left, and he still hasn't called like he said he would. Umma's been going back and forth between pacing around the apartment and listening to the radio. Finally, she took the remote control from Harabeoji and turned on the news. "For more updates," she said.

"Updates on what?" I asked.

"Just watch."

Sarah comes into the living room, all hurried, but she does a double take when she sees Umma sitting on the couch. "Hey. How come you're not at the store?"

"We closed early today," Umma says.

She doesn't explain more. Umma and Appa are kind of opposite in that way. Umma worries a lot, but in front of me and Sarah, she says everything is just fine no matter what's really going on. Even when she was cleaning up the broken mirror and she realized I saw everything, all she said was "Umma's so silly, huh? Good thing no one got hurt." When I asked if she was sure, she looked me in the eye and said, all firm, "Geokjeonghajima." She always says that. Do not worry. And that was that.

Appa's not as bothered most of the time, but when he is, everybody knows it.

"O... kay," Sarah says. Her eyes trail to the TV and she sits down on the couch next to me. The yellow plaid shirt she has tied around her waist bunches around her ankles as she pulls her knees into her chest. Whenever we watch anything, she sits like this, kind of cocoon-style. She has the same furrowed brow as Appa with the dent in the middle, except hers only appears when she's worried. It's there now, her eyes wide at the news footage. "I rushed home from volleyball practice to see this."

Of the hundred and one things Sarah is always up to, volleyball has been her favorite lately. She wants to be captain of the team one day because, of course, she's Sarah. If she does something, she has to be the best at it.

Harabeoji turns up the volume.

"It's not right, not right at all," a Black woman being interviewed by a news reporter is saying. You can tell she's seething with anger, but her voice is controlled, and she doesn't take her eyes off the camera, not once. "Where's the justice? Rodney King was beat up by four police officers and those cops just get to walk off, scot-free? No. No way. We all heard the verdict today. But we're here to say the verdict is wrong."

People are marching down the street with signs, shouting, "No justice! No peace!"

The sound rattles our living room.

"No justice!"

"No peace!"

"If we let this happen today," the woman continues, "it will keep on happening. That's a fact. And we won't have it."

The TV cuts to a grainy shot of a Black man being beaten up by cops with nightsticks outside his car. He's on the ground, face in the road, getting hit again and again and again, brutally, all over his body. They get him in the legs, the chest, even kicking him in the neck. He struggles to get up, but the cops keep on beating him with those sticks like they're really trying to kill him. My stomach churns. It's four against one with more officers just standing by, watching, and Rodney King is unarmed.

I've seen this on TV before, when the footage first came out last year. I remember feeling sick then too and Umma changing the channel, telling me not to look. I can feel her now, sitting to my right, her arm twitching like she wants to grab the remote and change the channel again. But this time we keep watching.

"On March third, 1991, this tape, provided by witness George Holliday, who captured the events on his video camera, was released of Sergeant Stacey Koon and Officers Laurence Powell, Theodore Briseno, and Timothy Wind using excessive force and brutality against motorist Rodney King," a news reporter states. Their mug shots flash across the screen, and from what I can tell, they all look white to me. "In addition to being shot with a Taser, King was struck by their batons upwards of fifty-three times."

The TV cuts to a photo of Rodney King after the beating, and I suck in a breath. His face is fractured and bruised, one eye dark red. The news reporter continues. "Today, at the trial in Simi Valley, all four officers were declared not guilty. Since the verdict was announced, unrest has been building in the city of Los Angeles. We cut now to live footage in South Central, where there have been reports of escalating violence."

The TV switches back to today. We're looking at a dusty street and I feel like I'm watching some kind of movie. Bottles being thrown at cars, smashing against windows, trucks doing U-turns and peeling away like they can't escape fast enough.

Wait.

I sit up straighter. "Did he just say South Central?"

That's where our store is.

As if reading my thoughts, Umma squeezes my hand and says, "Don't worry, Jordan. Your dad is fine."

"Huh?" Sarah turns to look at Umma. "What do you mean Appa's fine? Where is he?"

Umma pauses. I can almost see the wheels turning in her head, like she's trying to decide how much to share without freaking us out. "He went to go board up the store in case anything happens," she finally says. "But it's okay. Our store is far away from all of this. We're farther north, close to Koreatown, and this is Florence and Normandie. We're just being extra, extra careful."

She smiles and I know what's coming next.

Geokjeonghajima.

"Geokjeonghajima." She pats me on the shoulder and

then reaches over me to do the same for Sarah. But it doesn't make me feel much better, and by the look on Sarah's face, it doesn't do much for her either.

"Why hasn't he called, then?" I ask.

Umma thinks for a second and then nods. "Traffic. He's probably stuck in his car, still trying to get to Home Depot for supplies. Look at all these protestors." She shakes her head, making a disapproving noise. "Blocking up the roads. Don't they know people can't get home?"

"Umma," Sarah says in disbelief. "I think the roads are the least of anyone's problems right now. Don't you think it makes sense that people are mad about this? The Rodney King verdict is horrible."

"I never said don't be mad," Umma says. "And I never said it's not horrible. But what does this do? This violence? Who does it help? Anyway, I'm just saying, don't worry about your dad. Everything is fine."

Sarah looks back at the screen. "Not everything." She sighs and rubs her eyes with the back of her hand. "I just wish there was more we could do."

"Ya," Harabeoji says, startling all of us. "You just focus on yourself."

Sarah and I stare at him like he's grown another head that's started talking to us. I mean, he might as well have. He's not exactly an advice-giving kind of guy.

"In Korea during the war, if you stop to try to help others, you lose your own life," Harabeoji huffs. "So just do what you have to do for you."

Rude or not, I can't help but look at his missing fingers at that. Harabeoji doesn't talk much about the Korean War, but we know he lost those two fingers during a village bombing. The story goes that he lagged behind the other soldiers to stay close to his friend who was slower and weaker than the rest. When the village they were passing through was bombed, the soldiers at the very back were the ones hit the hardest. "Lucky I only lost this much," Harabeoji often grumbles. "The others weren't so lucky."

"Like your friend?" I asked.

"No. He was the luckiest. Left my side and ran away as soon as he saw me bleeding."

We all look at him now, waiting for him to say more, but he's done talking. Umma picks up the remote control and turns off the TV. The violence on the streets of South Central gets sucked away, just like that.

"Your grandfather is right," she says. "We didn't leave everything behind in Korea and come to America so you could get caught up in all these things. Right?"

Sarah looks down at her baggy jeans, picking at a fraying white thread. "Right," she says, but she doesn't sound very convinced.

"We came here for opportunities for both of you," Umma continues firmly. "So you can have bright futures and do anything you want to do and be anything you want to be."

My stomach sinks. For a minute when we were watching the news, I forgot about the suspension. But now it comes back, fresh and piercing like a bee sting.

They immigrated for us to have the chance to be something great, but what if all I amount to is nothing? Just like Appa already thinks.

A part of me is annoyed too. How's living in America automatically supposed to make you into somebody important?

"Look at the time," Umma says, rising from the couch. "Sarah, come help me with dinner."

The two of them walk out of the living room and Harabeoji shuffles out after them, leaving me alone. I grab the remote and turn on the TV again, lowering the volume so Umma can't hear.

The camera is still showing live footage from South Central. Now there are bricks being thrown through a shop window, glass raining down onto the sidewalk, crunching under people's feet as they run in and out of the store, arms full of liquor bottles. My eyes widen. The first thing I think is *Are they stealing?* The second is *What if that happens to us?* We have a liquor store just like that one. I wait for someone to come and stop them, but no one does. My throat gets tight. It's hard to breathe.

The news report switches to a bird's-eye view like they're filming from a helicopter. The camera's focused on a truck. At first, I don't know what I'm looking at, and then I see it. A group of four Black men are pulling a white man out from the driver's seat and beating him up, right there in the middle of the road. They're stepping on his neck, kicking him in the stomach, hitting him bloody, and my mouth is all dry, but I can't look away.

Someone hurls a cinder block at his head and I grab the remote and turn off the TV, my heart pounding so hard it's shaking me all over.

The phone rings.

I'm on my feet in two seconds, but Sarah's faster.

"Hello?" I hear her answer from the kitchen.

"Is that Appa?" Umma asks.

There's a pause. Then, Sarah's voice, saying, "Oh, hey. Um, okay sure. Just a second."

There's a shuffling sound like she's moving the receiver away from her mouth. She mumbles something to Umma and then yells, "Jordan, it's for you. But try not to hold up the line for too long, okay?"

I wipe my hands on my jeans 'cause they're all clammy before going to the kitchen to grab the phone from Sarah. I take it to my room, shutting the door behind me.

"Hello?"

"What's up, dude?"

It's my friend from church, Mike Rhee. Well. Kind of. Technically, Appa forbade me from hanging out with Mike after the Big Fight because "that kid's always making trouble." Appa's words exactly. He's never been a big fan of Mike and, I mean, I kind of get it. Mike's that kid who convinced half the youth group to skip out on Sunday service and instead climb up to the church rooftop to look for UFOs. He swore he saw one land up there. The adults freaked out when they found a bunch of kids on the roof, especially when one of the kids nearly fell over the edge. And the UFO he saw turned out just to be a Frisbee.

I haven't told Mike what Appa said, about me not hanging out with him anymore. I've just been keeping more distance lately, hoping he'll get the hint without me saying anything.

"Want to go over to Ben's place tonight to hang out?" Mike asks. His voice sounds eager, excited. "Hae Dang is driving me later. We can come pick you up on our way."

"I can't."

"Huh? How come? You didn't even ask your parents."

I sigh. I guess Mike hasn't really gotten the hint about me keeping distance. He keeps inviting me out to everything. To be honest, on another day, I might have been tempted to say yes. Ben's another friend from church who sometimes invites us over to play Super Nintendo. I know he just got *Super Mario World*. He was talking about it all last Sunday. But today is tense enough already without adding an extra reason for Umma and Appa to get upset with me.

"It's not really a good time to ask. My mom's in the

middle of making dinner and my dad's not home. He went to go board up our store."

"Really?" Mike says. "Oh, right—your store is in South Central, isn't it? Have you been seeing the news?"

My whole body tenses. Mike sounds worried now, and Mike never worries about anything. "Yeah. I have."

"Hold on, Hae Dang wants to say something to you."

There's a fumbling sound as the receiver's passed over and then Mike's older brother's voice comes through the phone. "Jordan?"

"Hi, Hae Dang," I say.

Hae Dang is the coolest guy I know. At least, that's what I think. Appa likes him even less than he likes Mike. "No wonder Mike is such a troublemaker," he's said. "Just look at his hyung."

Hae Dang is only seventeen but he already has a reputation for following nobody's rules but his own. One time, Mike told me that Hae Dang made fake IDs for all his friends so they could go gambling. He made this huge cardboard ID with the face cut out and all his buddies would stick their faces in the cutout hole and pose while Hae Dang snapped their photo and printed them out. I always wondered what the people working at the one-hour photo place thought when they got to his pictures. But knowing Hae Dang, he probably has someone who prints his photos for him in their own darkroom. He's connected like that.

The Rhee brothers don't care what anyone else thinks about them. Sometimes I wish I was more like that. I can act like I don't care about a lot of stuff but that's not the same as actually not caring. I bet if Mike went to my school, I wouldn't be the sixth grader that Mr. Martins sees the most.

"I heard your dad is out in South Central," Hae Dang says. "Just want to make sure you all know what's happening down there right now."

"We know," I say. The images of the man getting pulled out of his truck and store windows getting smashed with no one coming to help run through my head. "And he's okay. Our store's far from all that stuff." *For now, anyway*, I can't help but think.

"He's got a gun at the store, though, right? For protection."

A gun? My hands get clammy again.

"No," I say. "He doesn't. He doesn't use that kind of thing."

"It's not about whether you use it," Hae Dang says. "It's about not getting killed out there. You think anyone's going to mess with someone with a gun? I know I'd feel better with one."

"Jordan?" Umma calls from outside my room. "Are you still on the phone?"

"Listen, I should go," I say to Hae Dang. "We're waiting for my dad to call, so . . ." I trail off. And then because I don't know how to end the call, I just hang up.

I try to shake the feeling that Appa might not be okay. That something bad could happen to him or maybe already has. Umma said not to worry, but I know she's not taking her own advice. None of us are. Point is, he said he would call and he hasn't, and that's got us all on edge.

I stare at the phone in my hand. Come on. Ring. *Ring.*
It doesn't.

Hae Dang's words repeat in my head.

He's got a gun at the store, though, right? For protection. I know I'd feel better with one.

Thing is, Appa used to have a gun at the store. A lot of shop owners do, especially at liquor stores like ours. But he brought it home last year.

And I know exactly where he put it.

CHAPTER THREE

Appa brought his gun home the day after Latasha Harlins was murdered.

Latasha Harlins was a fifteen-year-old Black girl, shot in the back of the head by a store owner who thought she was stealing a bottle of orange juice. She died with the money in her hand that she was going to use to pay. It was messed up, really messed up. And the store owner? She was Korean.

Her name was Soon Ja Du.

We don't know her personally or anything, but it's weird how she could have been any one of the Korean church ladies we see every Sunday, wearing her best dress, or one of Umma and Appa's store owner friends working fourteen-hour days behind the counter. Maybe even Umma and Appa themselves, though I could never imagine them doing something like that.

When it happened, I heard our parents murmuring a lot, shaking their heads. "What a terrible, terrible thing. Why'd she do that? Why'd she kill that girl?"

Sarah was especially shaken by the whole thing. It hit her hard. "My age," she kept saying. "She was *my age*."

It shook me up real bad too. Umma didn't want me to see it, but I caught it on the news one time. The footage of Latasha getting shot. I wanted to throw up. I couldn't believe how fast it happened, how violent it was. Just a couple of seconds to take away someone's whole life.

Who shoots somebody like that, over a bottle of orange juice?

Who shoots a *kid* like that?

Here's another thing I remember. Latasha was killed just thirteen days after the video of Rodney King getting beat up by the cops was aired. Soon Ja Du was declared guilty, but instead of her going to jail, the judge let her off with a $500 fine, 400 hours of community service, and five years of probation. It's fresh in my head because just one week ago, I saw it all repeated on the news while Harabeoji was surfing channels. "Wasn't this a year ago?" I asked Sarah, who was sitting next to me on the couch.

"Yeah." She shook her head, her mouth set in a grim line. "But this is a new update. It's basically saying that the state agrees with the judge's decision. Soon Ja Du's sentence isn't going to change no matter how unfair people might say it is."

I think about the news, the protests, the anger, no justice no peace, and I get why everyone's so mad. They're mad about Rodney King, but they're also mad about Latasha Harlins, and I bet there's a lot more they're mad about too, stuff I don't even know about.

I stand in front of Umma and Appa's bedroom closet and pull the doors open, looking over my shoulder real quick to make sure I'm alone. I mean, I know I am. Umma and Sarah are busy making dinner and Harabeoji, last I saw on my way to my parents' room, is back in the living room, reading like he always does at this time of night, sitting on the floor with the book propped open in front of him. But still. I can't help but double-check just in case someone catches me doing something I shouldn't.

I reach into the back of the closet and wheel out Appa's old suitcase. It's heavy. Umma and Appa use their suitcases for storage, so it's packed with random things like old clothes and stuffed animals that we never got around to giving away or tossing out. I've never seen either of them use their suitcases for traveling. We don't really go anywhere, and we haven't gone back to Korea since we first moved to the States. There was that one time a couple of years ago, though, when we went on a family road trip to San Diego. Umma packed a rice cooker and a bunch of kimchi jars, so we ate most of our meals in the motel. I don't remember much else about that trip.

As silently as possible, I tilt the suitcase over so it's lying on its back and step on top of it like a step stool. I'm eye level now with the top shelf in the closet. There's more stuff up here, mostly family photo albums bursting with photographs, and a heavy pile of damyo, thick and heavy blankets printed with tiger faces and giant red roses. I push a big stack of albums aside. A bunch of loose photos slip out from between the pages and scatter onto the floor. I freeze for a second, listening in case someone heard me, but it doesn't seem like anyone did. I keep rummaging around until I find what I'm looking for.

A small black rectangular case tucked into the corner of the shelf.

I gotta jump a little to reach the handle, but I manage to grab it and pull it down from the shelf. I step down from the suitcase and sit on the floor, the case in my lap.

My heart is thudding so loud that I'm scared someone's going to hear me.

But no one does.

I open the clasps and lift the lid.

Appa's pistol stares back at me.

I've only ever seen it once before, the day he brought it home. I remember standing in the doorway of his room as he sat on his bed, unloading the gun in his hand, taking all the bullets out of the clip. When he looked up and saw me, I thought he was going to tell me to leave but instead he called me into the room.

"See this, Jordan?" he said. I remember he looked tired that day, more tired than I think I've ever seen him in my life. I remember thinking he should probably drink more coffee. "We keep this in the store in case there are any emergencies. Because we need to do everything we can to protect what's ours. But after seeing what happened yesterday..."

He went silent for a really long time, his palm closing over the bullets. I wasn't sure if I should say something to break the quiet so I just stood there, waiting.

"I don't ever want to do to someone what Du Soon Ja did to that girl," Appa finally said. He says it the Korean way— Du Soon Ja—with the last name first. He put the gun back in its case and then placed a hand on my shoulder, looking me hard in the eye. "I want you to understand something, Jordan. A gun is not a toy. I don't want to see you touching this. Do you hear me?"

"Yes," I said. "I hear you."

"Good."

He let me go, sending me out of the room. But as soon as I left, I stayed by the door, secretly peeking inside, watching as he opened his closet and slid the gun into the corner of the top shelf, safe out of reach.

I wonder now if Appa regrets bringing it home.

I know he said he'd never use it the way Soon Ja Du used it on Latasha Harlins and I know he would never. But then I think of that man who was pulled out of his truck and beaten up bloody with nothing to defend himself with. What if *he* had a gun? Would that have made a difference?

And what about those stores on the news that were being looted? Nobody was coming to help, but if there was someone inside with a gun, would it have changed anything?

Maybe. I think so. Isn't that what Hae Dang said? *You think anyone's going to mess with someone with a gun?* Just the sight of one might make people run in the opposite direction. Appa wouldn't actually have to use it or even come close to pulling the trigger. After all, he took out the bullets, and I don't know where he put them. It would just be enough to have it in his hand to scare away anyone who was coming for him or the store.

What if something happens to Appa and he has nothing to protect himself with?

Another scary thought hits me.

What if something happens to Appa and his last memory of ever talking to me is the Big Fight?

I feel a hot wave of shame now, remembering some of the things I said to him. Mean things. The kind of things you can't take back once they leave your mouth. And I never even tried to say sorry.

Something prickles in my throat like cactus needles

poking me from the inside. It feels like regret. Or maybe panic. Or maybe both.

I'll never forgive myself if that's the last conversation we ever have.

And then another thought hits me, so hard it makes me dizzy.

What if *I* bring the gun to Appa?

I know he told me never to touch it, but that was then and this is now. He didn't know that a day like this would come. What if he regrets bringing it home, needs it for self-defense, and I show up with it in my hands, ready to help protect us?

It wasn't just me that said things in the Big Fight that you can never take back. Appa did too. And one of the things he said, in a voice so loud it felt like a rockslide tumbling over my head, was this:

"You think of no one but yourself. Do you know how much we've sacrificed for you?"

And then this:

"You are my biggest disappointment."

Since that day, I feel like I've been buried in the rockslide, trying to figure out how to get out.

Maybe this gun is the way.

Immediately, I think of a hundred reasons why this is a bad idea. It's dangerous. What if someone gets hurt? How am I even going to pull this off? But in the back of my head, it's Mr. Martins's voice I hear in the moment he suspended me, what he said about my parents. *Well, they'll be so disappointed in you, won't they?*

Not if I can prove that I'm not a total failure.

Not if I can help.

I close the gun case and clasp it shut again. Then I pick up the phone on Umma's bedside table and dial.

Mike picks up on the third ring.

"Hey, Mike? It's Jordan," I say. "You still offering that ride?"

CHAPTER FOUR

Appa said he named me after a river.

The Jordan River is where Jesus got baptized, he said, and it's also what the Israelites crossed to get to the promised land. It symbolizes stepping into freedom and new beginnings. Being born again. He got this far-off look in his eyes when he talked about it, like he was thinking of his own crossing over the Pacific Ocean from Korea to America. "That's what you are for us," he said to me once. "The chance to be better."

No pressure or anything.

I always felt like the name was a jacket that didn't fit

right or shoes that were three sizes too big. I couldn't fill them. Couldn't even get close.

But today, for the first time ever, I feel like maybe I can.

I tell Mike I'll go to Ben's with him if he agrees to pick me up in thirty minutes. He does. Yeah, I know Appa told me not to hang out with Mike anymore, but I'm not really going to hang out. I'm not even planning on actually going to Ben's. I just need a ride to get close to our store.

Not that I mentioned any of that to Mike.

Or the gun. I didn't mention that either.

It's only when I hang up the phone that I realize it's one thing to make a plan; it's another thing to actually do it.

The gun sits on the carpet where I left it, safe in its case. I reach down and pick up the case, not sure how to hold it. I try cradling the case in my arms like a football and then with one hand around the handle, knuckles tight, my arm stiff and straight like I'm holding a briefcase. Neither feels right. Is it supposed to feel right to hold a gun?

I set the case down and open it up again, taking another look at the gun. I can't look away, but at the same time, it feels scary to be so close to one. The weird thing is, it kind of looks like the toy guns I used to play with growing up, but Appa was right when he said a real gun's not a toy. It's totally different up close. More serious. Dangerous. And even though I know it's not loaded, it still feels deadly. I hesitate and then pick up the pistol, carefully turning it over. It's heavier than I expect it to be and way too big. At least in my hands.

I'm not sure yet what I'm going to tell Mike when he gets here. Never mind Mike. What am I going to say to Umma and Sarah? What did I think I was going to do, just waltz out of the apartment holding Appa's gun, "I'll be back in an hour, don't worry about me?"

"Jordan!" Umma's voice calls from the kitchen. I nearly drop the gun on the floor. "Come eat!"

"Coming!" I call back.

I put the gun back in its case, clasping it shut. Then I quickly move everything in the closet back to where I found it, shoving photo albums into place, rolling suitcases upright. I nearly slip on the photos that fell from the albums earlier, and hastily grab them off the floor, stuffing them into the pocket of my jeans. No time to climb back on the suitcases and stick them in the albums.

Except for the empty space on the shelf where the gun

should be, it looks like I was never there. I close the closet and then slowly, slowly open the bedroom door, gun case in my hand. I look through the crack, silent, straining my ears to listen.

There's the sizzling of a frying pan, chairs being scraped back, metal chopsticks clinking against bowls as someone sets the table. Probably Sarah. It sounds like everyone is in the kitchen. I open the door wider, step into the hallway, and turn straight into the living room.

My red JanSport backpack is on the carpet where I took it off. I grab it now, shoving the gun case inside next to my Spanish textbook and Walkman, zipping it shut just as footsteps enter the room behind me.

I whirl around. Sarah stands there, arms folded, eyebrow raised.

"Didn't you hear Umma?" she asks.

"I did."

"Dinner's ready."

"I know."

She cocks her head to the side, inspecting my face like something's not right, like she knows I'm hiding something. But she doesn't look at my hands. She doesn't suspect the backpack. To her, it's just a normal bag. To me, it's the weight of the universe.

Before she can ask any questions, I push past her to the kitchen, stopping at my room to leave my backpack behind closed doors. Safe. For now.

Dinner is doenjang jjigae with bowls of white rice, still steaming hot. Squares of tofu and zucchini and mushroom slices bob up to the surface of the soybean-paste stew as Harabeoji sticks his spoon in, stirs, searching for the myeolchi hidden inside. I hate anchovies, but Umma always leaves them in the broth because Harabeoji likes to eat them. Nothing goes to waste around here, not even dried anchovy heads.

Umma lines the table with plates of banchan as we begin eating. She always tells us, "Meonjeo meogeo," urging us to eat first while she piles the table with more and more side dishes. Seasoned spinach, bean sprouts, kimchi, stir-fried cucumbers. When she's at work, she keeps the fridge stocked with containers full of banchan like this, and some kind of soup or stew in a pot on the stove for us to heat up while she's gone.

It's not every day we get to eat a dinner that she's just

cooked on the spot. But I'm so busy thinking about the backpack in my room and what's inside it that I hardly taste anything I eat. Everyone else is quiet too, like we're all scared that if we talk or even breathe too loud, we'll miss the phone ringing.

By the time we're done eating, Appa still hasn't called and my stomach feels like it's turning inside out.

I glance at the clock on the wall: 7:36 PM. Mike is coming in less than ten minutes. Shoot. I should have asked for more time.

Umma turns back to the counter to make more banchan. "So we're ready for tomorrow," she says, when what I think she really means is "So I can keep my hands busy. So I can show you that I'm not worried. So I can pretend everything is okay because if we're thinking about tomorrow, today must be fine." She turns on Radio Korea to listen as she cooks.

Harabeoji rises from the table and shuffles to the living room for his post-dinner nap on the couch. I leave the kitchen too, making a beeline for my room. I shut the door behind me, grab my backpack, sling it on, wonder if maybe I should take my textbook out—

Knock knock.

I jump so high, you'd think a ghost came through my door instead of someone just knocking on it. *Man, get ahold of yourself, Jordan.* I take my backpack off and open the door.

Sarah's standing on the other side. She tucks a loose strand of hair over her ear and puts her hands in her pockets. "Hey. Just wanted to see if everything is okay."

"Yeah. Why wouldn't it be?" My hand stays on the doorknob.

"I don't know," she says, and then she corrects herself, "Well, you know." She waves a vague hand in the air, half at me, half at nothing, or maybe it's the rest of the world, the staticky Korean voices coming from Umma's radio. She puts her hands back in her pockets.

"How's school?" she asks, switching gears.

I don't want to answer that question. I don't want to answer any questions.

"Fine," I say. Mike will be here any minute. "I have a big test coming up. I think I'm just going to stay in my room and study all night."

The lie comes easy, maybe too easy. *It's not too late to make that the truth*, a voice inside my head says. I don't know who that voice is. I think maybe it's the scared part of me.

"I can help you, if you need anything," she offers.

Having Sarah around is a lot like having two moms. When I was in kindergarten, Sarah was the one who would walk me home from school while our parents were at work. She would sit me down at the kitchen table with a box of Crayola crayons and get me to draw while she peeled fruit for my after-school snack. Sarah's not bad at a lot of things, but when it came to cutting fruit, she was terrible, constantly poking herself with the knife by mistake and crying because she hated seeing even a little bit of blood. But she did it anyway while I drew pictures of animals sitting in the grass—dogs, tigers, monkeys—the sky always one blue crayon line across the top of the page.

She's always keeping an eye on me, and ever since things went cold between me and Appa, she's only gotten more intense about it, like she thinks I need someone to make sure I'm doing okay at all times. It's annoying. I think sometimes she thinks I'm still in kindergarten.

"I'm good," I say. "Thanks, though."

I'm starting to feel kind of panicky. Time is ticking. Mike is coming. Maybe he's already here. What if I take too long and he decides to ring the buzzer? What if Umma answers, asks what he's doing here, and he tells her, "Jordan didn't say? He's going to hang out with me. He said so on the phone."

"Is that it?" I ask, wanting Sarah to leave.

She opens her mouth, hesitates, closes it again. Then she nods. "Yeah. If you change your mind, you know where to find me."

"Okay," I say, and then I close the door. I feel bad. But only for a second. I need to get moving.

I grab my backpack again and stand real still by the door, just listening to Sarah walk away. I hear her talking to Umma, voices muffled in the kitchen.

Now's my chance.

I slip out of my room, shutting the door softly behind me. Sarah will think I'm in here, studying. That's what she'll tell Umma. All I need to do is make it out the front door.

Suddenly, every creak in the floor sounds like a bomb going off. I can feel the weight of the gun as I move down the hallway, past the kitchen, holding my breath. *Don't look up. Don't see me.* Umma and Sarah are too deep in their conversation to notice me, the *chop chop chop* of vegetables against cutting board filling the air and masking my footsteps.

I pass by.

I quicken my steps, nearly jogging past the living room. I glance inside as I pass and, as I do, Harabeoji sits straight up on the couch with a gasp like a vampire rising from his coffin. His eyes lock on mine and my feet are glued to the floor.

It's over. I've been caught.

But then, just like that, his eyes grow cloudy with sleep and he's lying back down, murmuring to himself. I don't move, my heart loud in my ears like ocean waves. And then I go, as fast and quiet as I can, opening the front door, slipping out, closing it, running for the stairs, the gun in my backpack thudding against my back.

The outside air feels cool against my skin, and it's only then I realize how much I'm sweating.

I see Hae Dang's silver Toyota Supra pulled over on the side of the street, waiting for me. Hae Dang is in the driver's seat, wearing a white T-shirt and a baseball cap pulled low over his eyes. Mike is sitting next to him, his hair gelled straight up like a Troll doll, the opposite of his older brother's simple style. When it comes to hair gel, Mike never holds back.

"Jordan!" he calls, sticking his hand out the passenger window.

For a split second, that voice comes back in my head. *You could still turn around.* I think about doing just that, going back inside, and waiting for Appa to call instead of trying to help him myself.

I think about it.

But I don't do it.

Here's what I actually do.

I dive into the back seat and don't look back as we peel away from home.

CHAPTER FIVE

Hae Dang drives with all the windows down. He says it's because the air conditioner is broken and it gets too stuffy in here. At least, I think that's what he said. Honestly, it's kind of hard to hear with all the wind blowing and the radio playing. I take a deep breath, leaning my head back against the seat. I do it to try to calm myself down as we drive to the freeway, out of Glendale, past streetlamps and palm trees, but it doesn't help much. My stomach feels queasy.

Now that I'm sitting still, it really hits me what I'm doing. Have Umma and Sarah noticed I'm gone? Will they?

I stare at the back of Mike's head, his Troll hair pointing up over his car seat. I count all the things I've done today that would make Appa lose his mind.

Number one: get suspended from school.

Number two: sneak out of the house.

Number three: sneak out of the house with Appa's gun that I was told not to touch.

Number four: sneak out of the house with Appa's gun that I was told not to touch with Mike, who I was told not to hang out with.

Why did I think this was a good idea, again?

Somewhere in the distance, I hear sirens. I stick my head out the window to look, but I don't see anything. Wherever that siren's headed, though, it reminds me why I'm doing what I'm doing. Tonight's not like other nights. Appa needs me, and when I bring him the gun, he'll understand why I did what I did.

"You okay, Jordan?" Mike calls out. He points to the side-facing window, where I can see my face reflected behind his. "You're looking kind of green."

"I'm good," I say.

I hug my backpack tight against my chest, feeling the shape of the gun case inside. Music from the radio bounces my seat as we fight through the heavy freeway traffic. It's "Pass the Mic" by the Beastie Boys. Hae Dang is bobbing his head to the beat as he drives with one hand, fingers tapping against the steering wheel. Mike starts singing along, getting all the words wrong, knees jittering up and down. He's always full of energy, can't stop moving. Me? I'm so nervous, I'm barely paying attention to what's playing.

"Hey, Hae Dang?" I say. My voice comes out kind of squeaky and it makes Mike laugh. I clear my throat, try again louder. "Hae Dang?"

"Ya inma, I told you, you can call me Hyung," he says, not taking his eyes off the road. Hae Dang was thirteen when the Rhees immigrated to America, so he still has a bit of an accent. "What's up?"

Hyung is what Mike calls Hae Dang when he's speaking to him. It's the Korean way for younger guys to talk to their older brothers or older guy friends. Umma's always nagging me to call Sarah Nuna, the proper way for younger guys like me to refer to an older sister. I think I used to when I was little. I don't really remember when I stopped.

Maybe when we came to America and English became my main language. Anyway, it feels kind of clunky to me now since I don't use it at home, so I just nod at what Hae Dang said and go straight to my question.

"I was wondering if maybe you could drop me off at my family's store instead?"

He looks at me in the rearview mirror. "Your family's store? Why?"

"I, uh, need to give my dad something." I clutch my backpack tighter.

"What? I can't hear you."

"I said I need to give him something!"

Mike turns around in his seat, frowning. "I thought you were going to Ben's with me."

"I, uh . . ."

I probably should have mentioned it earlier. I mean, I know I should have. I guess I just didn't want to explain myself until I absolutely had to, but now I need to say something, and fast.

Before I can think of anything, though, Hae Dang is shaking his head. "I'm not driving to South Central right now. Didn't you hear what I said earlier? It's not safe there."

Oh.

Now I *really* don't know what to say.

He glances at me again in the mirror. "You want me to drop you back off at home?" He looks a bit annoyed. I should have thought this through more.

"No," I say quickly. And then again, more to myself, "No."

If Hae Dang isn't going to drive me to the store, I'm going to need to figure out another way to get there. The wheels in my head are spinning. Ben lives in Hollywood, on the outskirts of Koreatown. How far would that be from our store? Maybe I can walk. It's not too far from Koreatown, I don't think, but Hollywood might be a stretch. I wish I had a map. Why didn't I bring a map? Is there one in Hae Dang's car? Would it be weird to ask? I eye the glove compartment.

The drive is long, but it still feels like way too soon when the car rolls to a stop and Mike unbuckles his seat belt. We're here.

I follow Mike's lead and get out of the car, slipping my arms through my backpack straps. But as soon as I step out, I realize I've been so deep in my thoughts, I didn't notice where we ended up.

This isn't Ben's house.

This is Oliver's Burgers and Burgers, the restaurant Mike's parents own in Koreatown.

What are we doing *here*?

"I'll pick you up in half an hour," Hae Dang says through the open passenger window. He points a finger at Mike. "You remember the rules?"

"Yep," Mike says. "Don't waste time. Don't get hurt. Don't attract attention."

"Wait, what's going on? Where are you going?" I ask Hae Dang.

"I've got some stuff to take care of around the neighborhood. Just dropping you boys off. Taxi service." The way he says it, it sounds like "tax-shi suh-bee-soo." He grins and then nods at Mike. "Half an hour. Got it?"

"Yes, sir." Mike salutes. "Thanks, Hyung."

Hae Dang salutes back and drives off. I watch his silver car zoom down the street, turn a corner, and disappear.

I look at Mike. He looks at me. He's still jittery, knees bouncing up and down, even though there's no more music.

And then I look at Oliver's.

Oliver's Burgers and Burgers is small, kind of hut-like

with its sloped rooftop and brown brick walls. The sign is fluorescent, the lights flickering. I've been here a couple of times before with Mike after church. Every time I've gone, it's been busy. Kids with their grandparents, groups of teenagers, people sitting solo on the barstools. But today, I can see from out here that it's totally empty inside.

And completely dark.

"So are you going to tell me what we're doing here?" I ask. I can hear the confusion in my own voice.

Mike grins. "Just follow me."

"Wait—Mike—"

But he doesn't wait. He just takes a quick look over his shoulder before walking up to the glass front doors, locked behind a metal folding gate, fishing a bronze key out of his pocket. I let out a frustrated sigh and follow him to the doors. I can barely see anything inside the dark restaurant. Just the outline of seats, all empty.

"What's going on?" I ask. Something's not right. Now I look over *my* shoulder even though I don't know who I'm looking for or what we're even doing. When I look back at Mike, he's got both the gate and door open. He ushers me inside.

An alarm is going off in the restaurant. He runs to turn it off, calling to me, "Lock the doors, Jordan!"

He sounds so urgent that I do it right away. Only when the alarm stops and the restaurant is so quiet I can hear my own breathing do I wonder if maybe I should have run away instead.

I can see more now that I'm inside. From the light coming in through the glass front doors and the slivers through the window blinds, I make out the tile flooring, black and white, with brown cushioned booths lined up against the walls. Some of them are starting to look real old. Cracks form along the cushions with stuffing popping out. I look up and see a ceiling fan.

"Jordan!" Mike's voice calls out to me again, half shout, half whisper. "Can you come help me back here?"

I hesitate. I still don't know what's happening but being inside a dark restaurant with no one else around is giving me goose bumps. I can almost hear Appa's voice in my head. *That kid's always making trouble.*

Curiosity gets the better of me, though, and I follow Mike's voice to the back of the restaurant, past the cash register and into the kitchen. There's a grill, cold and still, and a big metal door that probably leads to the inside of a fridge. I pass it all, coming to a storage closet where Mike is standing inside, holding four fold-up chairs.

"What are you doing?" I ask. I look around for a light switch. "Where are the lights?"

"No lights. We don't want anyone looking in," he says. "Come on, help me with this." He hands me two of the chairs. I don't know what else to do so I grab them.

"Mike, I swear, if you don't tell me what's going on right now—"

"I will, I will. But it'll be easier to explain in a second. Follow me."

We carry the chairs back out to the front of the restaurant in darkness. He stops just below the ceiling fan and starts setting up the chairs, waving at me to do the same. He arranges them in a square formation with the seats facing each other and steps back to admire his work. He must like what he sees because he turns to me with a grin. Every time Mike smiles, I think of crocodiles, teeth sharp and pointy. I've thought so ever since we first met.

Mike was the new kid in Sunday school two years ago. His family had just moved to LA from Arizona. Right off the bat, here's what we all learned about Mike: He had a pet turtle named Wizard who he held on his lap during the entire road trip to California, and he loved to talk. A lot.

The other kids found him kind of annoying, but me, I was quieter than the rest of them and didn't have too many friends myself. So when Mike came along with his crocodile teeth, talking enough for the both of us, it was easy to become friends. He was funny and a little wild. He was always making some kind of plan inside his head.

Like now.

"So ...?" I say. "Are you going to explain what's going on?"

"Okay, so," Mike says. "I hid something up in the ceiling and I gotta grab it. But the other day, my dad fell off the ladder and it broke. I know, right? How cheap is that? Don't worry, my dad is fine. Anyway, I'm gonna need a boost." He pats the chairs. "You climb up here and then I'll get on your shoulders. I think that should be high enough for me to reach the ceiling. Oh, and keep watch. If you see anyone, do a birdcall."

"A birdcall? What are you talking about?"

"Okay, no birdcall, just say you see someone coming."

I'm barely keeping up with what he's saying, but then just like that, the pieces click together.

"Wait. Did you lie to me to get me to come *give you a boost*?" I say. I don't know whether I'm more angry or confused. Heat rises up my face. Angry. Definitely angry.

I grit my teeth, the gun weighing heavy on my back, fingernails digging into my palms. I should be on my way to Appa right now. Not here helping Mike with something so pointless. I think of the man on TV, pulled out of his truck and beaten senseless, and the stores being swarmed by looters with no one coming to stop them. Every second I spend with Mike is a second that Appa might be in trouble, might need the protection I have to give him.

"You said we were going to Ben's," I accuse.

He sighs a big sigh. "Come on, I'm sorry, Jordan. I knew if I told you I needed help, you wouldn't come. You never come out these days. I thought Ben's would be the most convincing invitation."

I open my mouth and look away. So I guess he *has* noticed I've been trying to keep my distance.

"You could've asked Hae Dang to help you," I say.

"He's got his own thing going on. I just bugged him for a ride."

"What thing?"

He shakes his head. "I don't ask him for details, he doesn't ask me. We don't have heart-to-hearts like you and Sarah."

"What?" I blink. "Me and Sarah don't have heart-to-hearts."

"Okay, if you say so."

"We *don't*. Anyway, that's not even the point!"

"Right. The point is, Hae Dang's got my back as long as I follow his three rules." He holds up his fingers. "You heard it, right? Don't waste time. Don't get hurt. Don't attract attention. He'll let me do what I need to do without asking questions as long as I stick by those rules."

Mike presses his hands together like he's begging. "Just do me this favor. Please? My dad closed shop early today 'cause he got all spooked about the riots. They're not even close to here. He's paranoid. He won't even let us sleep with the fan on in the summer 'cause he thinks we'll freeze to death or something."

I pause. "My mom says that too. Fan death. I think it's a Korean thing."

"Yeah. But my dad takes it to a whole other level. He threw out all our fans so we're not even tempted. Now he's sweaty all the time, just sitting on the couch in his white undershirt, sweating over everything." He makes a face. "Paranoid. But he did leave the restaurant empty, which means it's the perfect chance to get what I left here. And let's say he's right and people do destroy the place? Then this could be my last chance ever. So come on, we need to hurry before Hae Dang comes back for us."

It's my turn to sigh now, heavy and annoyed. "Fine. But," I add, thinking fast, "only if you promise to convince Hae Dang to drive me to my family's store after."

"Deal," Mike says immediately. He gestures to the chairs. "You go up first."

I climb onto the chairs, planting my feet on two of them. Mike climbs up onto the other two. "Ready?" he says, standing right behind me. "I'm going to get onto your shoulders."

"There weren't any better chairs than these?" I ask, the fold-up chairs wobbling a bit beneath my feet.

"Nope. My dad's office chair has wheels. And look

around you. The seating's all booths and stools nailed into the floor."

This has got to be the worst idea ever. Still, I squat down a bit, bending one leg and straightening out the other, planting my feet as firmly as I can. Mike puts his hands on my shoulders and places one foot on my bent leg. "You got me?" he says.

"Yeah." I hold on to his leg, steadying him as he pushes himself up off my thigh and onto my shoulders. I grunt, straightening up, swaying under his weight.

"Steady," he says, reaching for the ceiling. "My life is in your hands."

"You couldn't choose an easier hiding spot? How'd you get anything up there in the first place?" I ask. As annoyed as I am, I can't help but be kind of impressed at the same time. Who thinks of hiding something in the ceiling tiles of a burger restaurant?

"No duh, the point of a hiding spot is to make sure it's not easy," he says. "I snuck it up here while I was helping my dad dust the ceiling fan, back before the ladder broke." He grins, looking down at me. "It's not as easy, but it's kind of more fun this way, isn't it? We're like spies in a movie or something."

I roll my eyes. "Hurry up—you're heavy. What'd you hide up there, anyway?" I think of a treasure chest, a rooftop full of golden burgers.

"You'll see in a sec."

I keep one eye on the glass door, watching for movement. My shoulders are already starting to ache. Suddenly, I see something like a shadow and my whole body tenses up.

"I think I saw something."

Mike freezes. "What is it?"

"Oh. Never mind, it's just a bird."

"Man, shut up. You're making me nervous."

I watch as Mike reaches up, pushing one of the ceiling tiles up until he can shove his hand through. His tongue sticks out between his teeth in concentration while he searches for whatever he's looking for.

Then I see something coming straight toward the restaurant.

Not something. Someone.

And this time it's definitely not a bird.

"Mike."

"Almost got it."

"Mike!"

"What?"

"It's your dad!"

CHAPTER SIX

At first Mike's dad doesn't see us. He's just walking with his head down, digging in his pockets like he's searching for his keys.

He looks exactly like an older version of Hae Dang and Mike. Short and skinny, kind of like a bean sprout, and totally bald like one too. I see him around church sometimes, always talking and laughing. It's easy to recognize his voice 'cause he has a thick Busan accent and his laugh is the kind that booms from his belly. But I've seen him get serious with Mike a couple of times and it's like day and night. No more big booming laughs. Just a face that says *Don't mess with me.*

We have to get out of here.

"Hurry!" I whisper-shout to Mike. His hand's still in the ceiling and my shoulders are starting to shake from his weight.

"I got it!" He pulls his hand out, clutching something thick and bulky. Even without lights, I can see what it is. It's cash. A big wad of cash, tied with a rubber band.

He starts to put the ceiling tile back into place. I look at the door at the same time Mike's dad glances up from his pocket, a key ring in his hands.

First, he sees that the gate is open. Then he sees me. Or at least, he sees a shadow of me, something like a boy, two boys, in his restaurant in the dark searching through the ceiling tiles. He freezes for a second, like he's not sure what he's looking at. His face is all shock. And then it twists into something else and he's yelling. The sound is muffled through the glass door. He reaches for the back of his pants and pulls something out, something familiar, something that I also have sitting like a stone at the bottom of my backpack.

A gun.

My throat is dry. "Mike. Mike! We need to go!"

Mike glances at the door, swaying on my shoulders. And then everything happens at once.

There's a *bang!* and I shout so loud it feels like my heart is flying out of my throat, turbo speed. But it's not the gun. It's us, falling, losing our balance, and hitting the floor, folding chairs flying everywhere.

Mike goes down first, his ankle tangling with the chairs as he hits the ground hard. I manage to catch myself on my hands, but my palms and knees go skidding across the floor, burning my skin. But there's no time to think about the pain.

I hear the thud of the glass door as Mike's dad pounds his fist against it, still yelling. There's the frantic jingling of keys, like he's trying to look for the right one. And then it hits me. He won't find it because Mike took it. I take advantage of the moment, adrenaline pumping through my blood. I scramble up to my feet, grab Mike under the armpits, haul him out of the mess of chairs, and stand him up, swinging his arm around my shoulders.

Then we run. As fast as we can, past the cash register, the kitchen, the cold metal refrigerator door. We run with our arms around each other's shoulders like we're in some kind of three-legged race for our lives. I throw open the back door and immediately my nostrils fill with the smell of trash from the dumpster. We book it down the alleyway, zigzagging through back streets, trying to stay hidden as we get as far away from Oliver's as possible.

Mike hits his palm against my chest, telling me to stop. I do, and he collapses onto the ground, his back against the alleyway wall, panting. I lean over with my hands on my knees. I'm panting too, trying to catch my breath.

"Pretty sure you just broke all of Hae Dang's rules," I say.

"I know. Did you see that? My dad was going to shoot us!" Mike shakes his head. "I knew he was worried about the restaurant, but I didn't think he'd come back to protect it with a gun. He didn't even recognize it was us."

I feel suddenly sick. What if Mike's dad had had the right key in his hand, ready to go? Would he have swung the door open and taken his shots at us, believing we were robbers? And then another thought: Yeah, he didn't recognize us, but does that make a difference? What if we actually *were* strangers? Would that have made it okay to shoot?

Even if we weren't his son and son's friend, we're still some-body's son and somebody's friend, aren't we?

The weight of Appa's gun hidden in my backpack feels heavier than ever. I slump down next to Mike. His hand's covering his ankle and he's wincing.

"Are you okay?" I ask, remembering the fall. I look down at my own hands, wincing too, the skin peeling from where I went skidding.

"I think so," he says. He pulls his hand back and rolls up the leg of his cargo pants. I inhale through my teeth.

His ankle's swollen and it looks like it's still swelling, like a balloon slowly being filled with helium, getting big enough to float off into the sky. His skin's bright pink like the inside of a grapefruit cut open, shiny and raw. I look away.

"At least he didn't shoot straight through the windows," Mike says with a shaky laugh. "We just got them cleaned last week."

I laugh along even though I don't really feel like laugh-ing at all.

We fall into a sort of silence, just listening to cars zoom

by. I realize I don't know what to do now. The gun's still in my backpack. I could try to walk to our store.

But what about Mike? I can't just leave him here.

Or can I?

I don't owe him anything. We could go our separate ways. He could try to get in touch with Hae Dang somehow, get a ride home. Besides, *he* tricked *me* into coming along with him and getting involved in the first place. Appa was right. Trouble does follow him, and it's not my job to take care of him. My job is to get to Appa as soon as possible.

You weren't exactly honest with him either, that voice inside my head says. *You didn't plan on hanging out. He doesn't know about the gun in your bag.*

My face feels hot as I try to push that voice down. I don't want to think about it.

My mind goes back to the image of Mike's dad holding a gun. It feels different, suddenly, trying to bring a gun to Appa after seeing someone else hold one, ready to shoot. It feels more . . . I don't know. Real.

But I'm already out here. I've come this far. And it's

different, what I'm trying to do with this gun. I'm trying to protect Appa. I'm not trying to shoot anybody. It's different.

I realize Mike has been talking this whole time and I haven't heard a word he's saying.

"Better than when I broke my arm. You remember, right? When I had to wear that nasty cast for a month? That was definitely way worse. This is nothing. Probably just twisted."

He's talking a lot, maybe trying to distract himself from how big his ankle's getting. Now that I think about it, I can't believe how far he ran on it. It looks painful. Really painful.

How can I leave him like this?

"Come on," I say. I get up, holding my hand out to him. "Let's go find help."

>>>>

We walk down Vermont slowly, Mike limping, me keeping his arm around my shoulders. We pass by convenience stores, laundromats, restaurants selling kalguksu and naengmyeon, some open, some closed. For the ones that are closed,

I wonder if it's because it's after hours or because they flipped the sign early, worried about everything happening just a neighborhood away. I'm not sure what time it is, but if I had to guess, it'd probably be around 8:30 now. There aren't a lot of people on the street. I can't help but wonder if Umma's noticed that I'm gone yet. I push the thought out of my head. I don't want to think about it.

I don't even know what finding help looks like. I keep my eyes out for a pharmacy or something, unsure, nervous to go into any store with the gun in my backpack. What if someone sees it? I feel like everyone will know just by staring at my face. *That kid has a gun! You can see it in his eyes!*

Mike suddenly stops so I stop too. Maybe he needs a break.

And then he mutters, "There's a cop."

I turn my head to the side and see that he's right. There's a police car just around the corner with a cop standing by it, talking into some kind of walkie-talkie. Mike straightens up a bit, dropping his arm from my shoulders like he doesn't want to stand out for any reason. I realize we both have things we wouldn't want that cop to see. Mike with his wad of cash. Me with my gun.

Even without those things, seeing a cop is the last thing I want to do.

One time years ago, around the time we first came to LA, we lived in a first-floor apartment that was robbed. Umma's wedding ring was gone, and our TV. Our neighbor called the cops for us, and when they came—there were two of them—they stomped into our home with their boots on, firing question after question to my parents, who could barely keep up with all the English words being thrown into the air. In the end, they left and Umma spent an hour on her knees, scrubbing the carpet with a toothbrush, trying to get the dirt stains out that their shoes left behind. Her wedding ring was never found.

Right after that was when Appa got the gun to protect our store. "Because if anything bad happens, the cops aren't going to help us," he said. "We have to be ready to help ourselves."

My parents couldn't talk to the police here, and back in Korea, the cops were known for taking bribes, so they had a lot of reasons not to trust them. Because they didn't trust the cops, I didn't either. And watching the news today with the footage of Rodney King, it's hard to know how we're ever supposed to.

"Be cool," I mutter to Mike.

We walk by as casually as possible. Nothing suspicious to see here. Just two kids walking down the street. Just when we've passed him and I'm starting to relax, the cop shouts, "Hey! You dropped something!"

My heart sinks. I immediately crane my head to look at my backpack, as if expecting to see a huge hole in the bottom where the gun fell through. But there's no hole and I can feel the gun case still safe in my bag. So then . . . I look at Mike, my stomach sinking. Did he drop his cash?

But it's not that either. The cop walks toward us, holding out a crumpled photograph.

"This yours? It fell out of your pocket."

Oh shoot. It's one of the photos I picked up from Umma and Appa's closet. Of course it would choose now of all times to fall out of my pocket. Worst. Timing. Ever.

"Yes, sorry," I say, grabbing the photo from the officer's hand, my face flushed.

He looks back and forth between me and Mike, frowning.

He's got hair so blond it looks almost white. I hold my breath, trying to look as innocent as possible.

"It's not safe to be out and about tonight, especially for kids like you," he says. "What are you doing out here?"

"We were just on our way home," Mike replies easily. "It's not far from here."

The officer opens his mouth, but his walkie-talkie beeps, interrupting him. "All right, then, get going," he says, distracted, answering the call. "And stay out of trouble!"

"Yes, sir," Mike and I both say.

And then we go on, my heart thudding in my chest.

Only when we turn around and see that the officer is gone does Mike sag against my shoulders again, grimacing. "I think I'm going to need a break soon," he says. We walk even slower than before, turning onto a residential street lined with houses. They look like they used to be pretty nice, but the walls are all plastered with stucco now and it's got a more run-down feel to it. We go until it's quiet—no more cops or restaurants or cars from the main street—and then we sit down on the sidewalk, under a streetlamp.

Mike stretches his leg out. "That feels much better," he sighs, wiggling his toes. "Not broken at least."

"Good," I say. I let out a deep breath. "We got lucky that cop was distracted."

"Yeah, lucky. Probably helps that we look the way we do too."

"Like kids?"

"Yeah. Asian kids." Mike shrugs. "Hae Dang's always talking about that. How if you're Asian, people think you're good and quiet and expect you to stay out of the way. To know your place. Unless you look like you're in a gang. Then all bets are off. Hae Dang talks a lot about that too."

That makes me pause. I didn't really think about that at first, but now that I am, I can't help but wonder. Did the cop let us go so easily because we're Asian? Did that have anything to do with it?

"So." Mike nods at the photo I'm clutching in my hand, changing the subject. "You just keep random pictures in your pocket or something? You really had to drop it right in that moment, huh?"

"It's not like I meant to," I say, defensive. I unclench the photo from my fist, smoothing it out on my knee.

"Aww, is that little naked baby Jordan?" Mike coos, peering at the photo.

"Shut up," I say, my ears flaming.

It is baby me, though, lying butt-naked on a blanket with Appa sitting next to me, laughing with a book in his hands. Man. He looks so much younger here. I mean, I do too, but that's obvious. I can't even remember the last time I saw Appa laugh like that.

I take a closer look at the photo, pointing at the book. "My dad used to read to us from this book of poetry every night. It was his favorite."

Mike squints at the picture. "Doesn't look like a book of kids' poems to me."

"Nah. It was for adults. I didn't understand a word of it." I laugh. "But he kept at it for a while. He was really into that stuff. Even wrote some himself, I think."

"He should've been a poet, then," Mike says.

"Maybe." All of a sudden, I feel kind of sad. I completely forgot that Appa used to love poetry. He really wanted me and Sarah to love it too. I think he also thought that reading to us from this book would help us remember Korean after we moved here. But it's been a long time since he's read to us—a couple of years, maybe more—and I don't even know the last time I caught him sitting by the window after coming home from work, scribbling in the notebook he kept on his bedside table. I haven't seen that notebook in a long time either.

"Anyway." I shove the photo back in the pocket of my jeans. I'll have to move all the pictures to my backpack later so they don't fall out again, but I'll do it when Mike's not looking. I don't want him to accidentally see what else is in my bag. "We should get going. You up for it?"

He looks down at his ankle, tries rolling it. "I don't know. Might be kind of hard."

I chew my lip. Maybe I *should* have just left Mike behind earlier. I need to get to Appa as fast as possible and it won't help if we have to stop every ten minutes so Mike can rest his foot.

"You can carry me?" Mike suggests.

"You're not getting on my shoulders again."

He snaps his fingers. "We find a skateboard to steal."

"Yeah right."

"You're no fun."

I look around, feeling frustrated. There's got to be a way we can get Mike moving faster.

My eyes fall on the tree in the yard we're sitting in front

of. Hmm. The branches look low enough for me to grab if I jump. I walk up to it, take a quick look at the house to make sure no one's watching from the windows, and jump, grabbing for a longer branch. It cracks but doesn't snap off the way I want it to.

"Uh, what are you doing?" Mike asks.

"What do you think?" I say, jumping again, the tree rustling. "I'm trying to get you a cane."

"A cane?" He cracks up. "That's your idea? I still think my skateboard idea is better."

"Yeah, well, you can't always steal things to help you out." I stop jumping to look at Mike. "Are you going to tell me where that money's from?"

"Huh?"

"The money from Oliver's." I've been wanting to ask ever since I saw him pull out that wad of cash. Money doesn't just come out of ceilings like that, and I know for a fact that Mike doesn't have a job. I mean, he helps out at the restaurant here and there, but if it was cash from that, he definitely wouldn't be hiding it.

"I stole it from the cash register." He says it plain, completely honest. "I've been taking a little bit here and there and keeping it in my room, but then my dad started noticing the numbers were off so I needed a new hiding spot. He's so suspicious, my dad. I gotta stay careful."

"You take money from your parents' restaurant?" I don't try to hide the surprise in my voice. I picture stealing something from my parents' liquor store. I can't even imagine taking a stick of gum.

He shrugs again. "You asked."

We're silent for a second. And then I jump again, reaching for the branch, and ask, "What are you going to do with it? The money."

"Not sure," he says. He shoots me a big grin. "Maybe buy my friends some burgers."

"You're kidding." Jump. Grab. Miss.

"Why kidding?"

"You're really stealing money from your parents' burger place to buy more burgers?" The branch cracks a little more. Almost got it.

"It's just one of the options," he says. "I don't know. Maybe I'll get Wizard a new tank."

"He's still alive? That turtle is ancient."

Mike laughs and then goes kind of quiet. "You know

what my mom always says to me? She says money is freedom. That having lots of it is the American Dream. I don't want to wait till I'm old to be free or to live the dream. I want to be free now. So." He pats his pocket. "Now I can be."

I leap up and grab the branch with both hands, and this time the whole things snaps off. Mike cheers, and I raise the branch over my head like a trophy, laughing triumphantly.

"Now let's get out of here," I say.

But before we can say or do anything else, there's the sound of a door swinging open and a pool of rectangular light falls over us from behind.

"You kids!" a voice yells. "What are you doing on my lawn?"

CHAPTER SEVEN

I whirl around. Mike tries to jump up but then falls back on his butt, his ankle throwing him off-balance. A tall Black man walks out of the house, older than Appa with hair that looks a little gray, but a little younger than Harabeoji with shoulders that still look sturdy and not at all stooped. He has such a deep frown on his face that even from far away, I can tell he's seriously annoyed.

"This is private property," he says. His voice is all deep, all warning, and his eyes narrow at the branch in my hands. I gulp.

"Uh, I can explain—" I start.

"Wait, I know you!" Mike says. He struggles up to his

feet and hobbles to where I'm standing under the tree. "It's me. Mr. Rhee's son! From Oliver's Burgers and Burgers."

The man's face goes from angry to kind of exasperated. I've seen that look before on my principal's face. That *You again? Of course it is* expression.

"You know him?" I say to Mike.

Mike nods. "He's a regular at Oliver's. Lots of people around this neighborhood are. Aren't you, Mr. . . . uh . . . Mr. . . . ?"

"Mr. Gary," he huffs. "And I used to be a regular. It's been a while now."

"We were just on our way," I say, taking a few steps back. I've got to get us back on track to get to Appa.

"Oh no you don't," Mr. Gary says. "First, you're going to explain what you're doing out here, vandalizing my property. Second, you're going to apologize for nearly waking up my wife, who's trying to sleep off a migraine. You're lucky it's me out here and not her because you do *not* want to be the one to wake her up right now."

"S-sorry," I stammer, clutching the branch. "It's just, my friend here, he hurt his ankle and we needed a cane so . . ."

Even to my own ears, the story sounds weak. I look to Mike for help.

"Um...uh..." For a second Mike looks unsure, and then he collapses to the ground, clutching his ankle with a howl so loud it makes both me and Mr. Gary jump.

"It hurts!" Mike cries. "It hurts so much. I—I think I may have to get surgery. Or a new ankle. What's that word? Where you have to get surgery to replace an old thing with a new thing?"

"Transplant?" I say.

"Yes. Yes!" He groans. "I need an ankle transplant!"

"For God's sakes, be quiet!" Mr. Gary says, shushing us and throwing a look over his shoulder, probably making sure we haven't woken up his wife with Mike's hollering.

"I'm just saying, Mr. Gary, we had no choice but to do what we did," Mike says. "Just take a look for yourself."

Mr. Gary sighs, heavy, and walks over to us, grumbling, "I swear, if you kids are pulling my leg..." He crouches down to look at Mike's ankle and his eyes go all big. "Well, now, that's ugly, isn't it?"

"I mean, I wouldn't go that far," Mike says, offended.

"See?" I say, already starting to step away again. "We weren't lying. So we'll just get going now. Sorry again about the tree and your wife and all that."

Mr. Gary inspects Mike's ankle a little closer and shakes his head. "You're going to want to ice this and bandage it up immediately. A cane alone won't do you much good."

"Any chance you could help with that?" Mike asks hopefully.

"Mike," I say, shooting him a look. "We gotta go."

Mr. Gary grimaces like he'd really rather not be bothered by this, but he stands up and helps Mike to his feet. "Fine," he says. "But only if you promise to stay quiet."

"I can do that," Mike says, following Mr. Gary into the house.

"Mike!" I say. I can't believe this. Every minute we spend here is a minute we could be getting closer to Appa. Frustration presses against my chest.

Maybe I'm being selfish. I mean, I know I kind of am. After all, Mike's the one that's hurt. But nobody told him to hide his money in the ceiling in the first place. This isn't what I came out here to do tonight.

"Come on, Jordan," Mike says, turning around and

gesturing for me to follow him. "It'll just take a few minutes. And it'll be faster in the long run. I'll walk better once I'm patched up."

I take a deep breath. Okay. Fine. Maybe he's right. "Only a few minutes, then," I mutter. I leave the branch propped up against the tree and follow him inside.

As soon as we enter the house, we're in Mr. Gary's living room. The first thing I notice are the photos on the walls. There are lots of them. Pictures of Mr. Gary and his wife, their kids, and what looks like their kids' kids. He's got a big family. There's a clock on the wall too and it hits me that it's already past nine PM. My stomach sinks. It's getting real late. Who knows what might have happened to Appa during all this time?

The second thing I notice is the birdhouses. There are a lot of them. All shapes and sizes, lined up in a row next to a bunch of tools on the wooden coffee table, spilling over onto the carpeted floor next to the brown couch in the corner. Some done, some almost done, all in different shapes and sizes.

I've never seen anything like it.

Finally, my eyes land on the TV. The news is playing. The

volume's turned way down, but the screen is bright with fires, so bright I can almost hear the crackling flames in my ears. I can't take my eyes off the burning buildings and suddenly, I feel a bit sick. I've never seen anything like that either.

Was this happening right now? While I was putting Appa's gun in my backpack, standing in the dark in Oliver's Burgers and Burgers, running through the alleyways, talking to a cop—was the city being set on fire?

"Get that ankle elevated," Mr. Gary instructs Mike as he disappears somewhere inside the house. His voice shakes me out of my thoughts, bringing my eyes off the TV.

For a second, I turn my head to the open door, smelling for fires. But I can't smell anything. I help Mike over to the brown couch, stepping around the birdhouses on the floor. He lies back and lifts his ankle onto a cushion.

"Could you help me take my shoes off?" he asks.

I do, and up close again, I can see that his ankle has gotten worse. I feel a twinge of guilt at how frustrated I was about him wanting to come inside for help.

"Yo," Mike says, looking me in the eye, all serious. "What I said out there made me think. What if I really do need ankle surgery?"

"For real?" I say, sitting down next to his foot. "I don't even know if you're joking." I take off my backpack, holding it on my lap. My eyes drift back to the TV.

He sighs, staring up at the ceiling. "I liked my ankle. I liked my whole foot, really."

"This kid's dramatic, isn't he?" Mr. Gary walks into the living room, holding a bag of frozen peas in one hand and a bandage roll in the other. He throws the bag of peas to me and I barely have time to catch it before it hits me in the face. "Ice it," he orders, pointing at Mike's foot.

I press the peas against Mike's ankle. Mr. Gary comes over to the couch and I squeeze one arm around my backpack, anxious about what's inside. Whenever I think about the gun resting in its case against my Spanish textbook, it feels like another stone drops into the pit of my stomach. And I've thought about it a whole lot since leaving my apartment. That must mean there's a whole mountain of stones in me now, just piling on top of each other.

Mr. Gary doesn't notice though. Just like everyone else, all he sees is a regular backpack next to a not-so-regular-sized ankle, which is where his eyes go. He crouches down next to Mike's foot and takes a look, touching it gingerly.

"Ow!" Mike cries.

"I told you to be quiet," Mr. Gary says, giving Mike a warning look. "Seems like you may have a sprain."

He unrolls the bandage in his hand, starts wrapping it around Mike's foot. He raises his eyebrows at both of us as he works. "So you two are really going to make me ask?"

Mike and I exchange glances. "Um, right," I say. "My name's Jordan. And you already know Mike."

"Not your names," Mr. Gary huffs, rolling his eyes. "I want to know what two young kids are doing out at night during a state of emergency, one of you with a golf ball growing out of his ankle."

"It looks like a golf ball?" Mike says at the same time I say, "State of emergency?"

"Mayor Bradley officially declared it," Mr. Gary says. His body kind of stiffens as he nods toward the TV. "There's an uprising. People are rioting. Looting stores, setting them on fire. It's dangerous out there."

An uprising. I think of the news footage from earlier today. The marching, the looting, no justice no peace, cans and bottles bouncing off car windows, the man from the truck. My arm tightens around my backpack again. I was already feeling like I had to get to Appa as fast as possible. But if things are getting worse out there—if people are rioting and setting stores on fire like Mr. Gary's saying and the news is showing—that means I need to get to him even faster. I need to get him the gun for protection from who knows what he could be facing out there.

I ignore the stones tumbling around my stomach. No matter how heavy I feel, I know I have to do this. I have to protect him and I have to prove that I can.

I have to.

I have to.

You think of no one but yourself. I hear Appa's voice in the back of my mind and I shake my head, chasing it out. I'll show him it's not true.

Don't worry, Appa, I think. *I'm coming.*

I tune back into the conversation, realizing that Mr. Gary is still waiting for an answer about what we're doing outside and Mike is trying to field it. "We were on our way home when I fell," he's saying. "We don't live too far. We were nearly almost there when I just couldn't walk anymore."

"Hmm," Mr. Gary says like he doesn't really buy it. He tightens the bandage around Mike's foot, finishing up.

"You're good at this," Mike says.

He grunts. "I have five kids. Four played sports growing up. Not the first sprain this house has seen."

The whole time he's been fixing Mike up, I've been holding the bag of frozen peas, slowly melting in my sweaty hands.

"I hope someone knows where you are," Mr. Gary says sternly.

"Yes," I say when really I mean no.

"Definitely," Mike says when really he means absolutely not.

"Hmm," Mr. Gary says again.

Mike wiggles his toes and swings his legs off the couch, sitting up. "Thanks so much. This feels way better already." He grins. "Could I maybe ask for one more favor?"

Mr. Gary narrows his eyes. "You like to push your luck, huh?"

"I was just going to ask if I could use your phone," Mike says. "To let my parents know we're still on our way."

Mr. Gary sighs and I know he can't say no to a kid

asking to call his parents. "Down the hall, to the left. And remember—"

"Yes, yes, I'll be quiet."

Mike limps out of the living room. I wonder who he's going to call. I highly doubt it's actually his parents. I think of the image of Mr. Rhee through the glass door, holding a gun, and I shudder.

"Now what's wrong with you?" Mr. Gary asks. "You got the chills?"

Nothing gets past him. "No. I'm just, uh . . ." I look for a distraction and point to the TV. "The fires. They're out of control, huh?"

He heaves himself onto the couch next to me, staring at the screen. His expression is unreadable. I can't tell if he's sad or angry or nothing at all.

"They are," he says.

I think of what Umma said when we were watching the footage of South Central. *But what does this do? This violence? Who does it help?* Looking at how bad things are getting, I can't help but wonder the same thing, can't help but worry about Appa caught somewhere out there, can't help but think out loud.

"I know people are mad," I say. "But does this really help make them feel better?"

Mr. Gary is quiet for a long time. Finally, he looks at me, a different kind of expression on his face. A complicated one. If before I thought his face said nothing, now I get the feeling that it says everything. All the sadness, all the anger, all the heavy feelings in the world.

"Jordan, you said your name was. Right?" he says.

I nod.

"You know how long I've been going to Oliver's Burgers and Burgers? Since Mr. Oliver himself opened it."

I blink. I didn't even know Oliver was a real person. I always thought it was just a name.

"Our whole family loved it. It was our place to go for special occasions, like after a good game or when the kids got a great report card. A tradition of sorts. We would get the Supreme Deluxe Burger with all the dipping sauces on the menu for their fries. Of course, we went on non-occasions too, but we didn't dare eat that Supreme Deluxe on any regular day. Eventually, Oliver sold the business to another owner. And then that owner to another owner. Your friend's father."

"Mr. Rhee," I say.

"Yes. Throughout the ownership changes, we kept up our tradition of going to Oliver's even though it wasn't really Oliver's anymore. But it hasn't been the same. Lots of Black families stopped going and I can see why."

"Is it the burgers?" I ask.

He shakes his head. "The burgers are fine, though nothing beats Oliver's original. But no. It's just not the same when each time your family goes there, the cashier takes an extra five minutes to count out every cent of what you paid to make sure you're not trying to cheat them. When the owner himself comes out to watch us while we eat and usher us out when we've barely finished, saying there's people waiting for our table when nobody is.

"What I'm saying is this. We don't find joy in burning the city," he says. "We find joy in joy. But it's hard when they keep stealing it from you. In everyday ways while you're trying to eat with your family, and in ways that make the news and give my wife a migraine that lasts for days. You're familiar with what happened with Rodney King and the verdict that was announced today, yes?"

I nod. "Yes."

"A man recorded what happened with his video camera, so we all saw it with our own eyes," he says. "But even before there were cameras, before the public was watching, there has been a long, long history of police violence against Black people. These protests? This uprising? It's not just about today. It's about all those lifetimes of injustice that have gone unheard." His voice catches in his throat. "You'd think the footage would be enough. We all saw the truth. But it wasn't. They won't let us have a moment to breathe."

I'm quiet this whole time, turning over Mr. Gary's words in my head. The *we* he's talking about are Black people, but who's *they*? I think of the four police officers beating Rodney King. *They* could be white people or the cops. And then I think of Soon Ja Du pulling a gun on Latasha Harlins. Could *they* be Korean people too? Could *they* be us?

I get the feeling that *they* is everything I'm thinking of but more. A hundred times more, a thousand times, a million. I get the feeling that Mr. Gary can think of lots of examples when he thinks of *they* while I can only name a few, that *they* is something bigger than I really understand right now, sitting on his brown couch, still holding that bag of peas.

I hand it back to him because I'm not sure what else to do. I wish I knew what to say. He takes the bag of peas, sets it down on the table next to his birdhouses. And then Mike enters the living room, flashing us a double thumbs-up.

"Done with the phone call," he says. "Thanks again for everything, Mr. Gary."

Mr. Gary puts his hands on his knees, rising from the couch. "All right," he says, all stern again. "You said home wasn't far from here? Get going, then. And stay alert."

"Yes, sir," Mike says, putting his shoes back on.

"Yes, sir," I say as well. I put on my backpack and take one last look at the TV. The screen's not showing fires anymore. It's cut to a news reporter. I want to hear what she's saying, but the volume's still too low, so instead I follow Mr. Gary to the front door.

Mike and I thank him again as we walk out of the house. "Is it okay if I take this?" Mike asks, pointing to the branch leaning against the tree.

"Might as well—you've already gone and damaged the poor tree," Mr. Gary says, shaking his head with a frown.

We're almost to the sidewalk when I pause, turning around.

"Mr. Gary?" I say.

"What is it, kid?"

"What's with all the birdhouses?"

At this, he smiles for the first time during our whole visit. It's slight, barely there, but it's still a smile. "My grandkids like them. They're a little younger than you."

I nod, wondering if he helped Mike because he thought of his grandkids when he looked at us. "That's cool."

I still wish I had something better to say, but that's all I can think of for now. As we walk down the street, I turn back once or twice, each time noticing that he's still standing in the doorway, making sure we're on our way home, until he can't see us anymore.

CHAPTER EIGHT

Mike's still slow, but he's a lot better than before. Between the bandage and the branch cane, he's doing okay walking along on his own. He seems happy too. "We got lucky," he keeps saying. "Real lucky."

"Yeah," I say, and I mean it. I do. Except now that we're back on the streets, all I can think about is how I need to get to Appa right away. I can't get the image of the fires out of my head. I look helplessly at the street signs, feeling unsure what to do or how to get to the store.

"Man, how many birdhouses do you think he had in there?" Mike is saying. "I think I counted at least twenty."

"Yeah," I say again, distracted.

I should have asked Mr. Gary for a map. But he would have asked why, and we already told him that we were on our way home, that we live close by. Why would we need a map?

"I wonder what his job used to be. I bet he was some kind of carpenter."

I don't answer.

"Jordan? Come on, imagine it. Do you think he went to carpentry school and became like a birdhouse master? Are there classes just for birdhouses? I feel like that could be a fun thing to learn. We should go back one day and ask him to teach us."

Frustration bubbles up in me and I turn to Mike, sighing loud. "Mike, aren't you even a little worried right now? Do you know where we are? Do you know where we're going?"

Mike blinks. "Of course I know. Where do you think I've been leading us this whole time?" He smooths up his hair, which is starting to droop a bit. "I sent a message to Hae Dang's pager when I was using Mr. Gary's phone. I asked him to pick us up at Silver Star Karaoke. And before you say anything, yes, I know how to get there. Relax, okay? I know Koreatown."

My mouth falls open. I don't know what I'm more

surprised about. The fact that Mike has a plan that involves meeting Hae Dang at a noraebang or that he's so sure of where we are. I don't know why either of those things surprises me exactly. Mike always has ideas, from climbing church rooftops to hiding cash in the ceiling of his burger place, and this *is* the neighborhood where his family's restaurant is. I guess I've just never really thought of his plans as helpful before.

He keeps walking. I follow after him.

"How'd you say all that through a pager? I thought you could only send numbers."

"We have a code for different places in Koreatown. Five-five-one-one is Silver Star Karaoke. Two fives because they look like the letter *S*, and eleven because *K* is the eleventh letter in the alphabet. I've used the code before when I needed to let him know where I was."

"You guys have your own code?" I'm impressed. "Man, why didn't you say so earlier? The first thing we would've done is find a pay phone."

He rolls his eyes. "Sorry if I wasn't thinking straight—my life was kind of on the line." He gestures down to his ankle. "In case you forgot."

Mr. Gary was right. He is dramatic. "Why are we meeting Hae Dang at the noraebang of all places?" I ask, suddenly suspicious. Mike's not planning on getting us a room so we can spend an hour singing, is he? That would be just like him.

"We know the family who owns it," Mike says. "There's a hyung we know, Brian, who usually works there at night. It's not too far from where we are now and far enough away from Oliver's." He makes a face. "Don't want to run into my dad again tonight, you know?"

"Right."

There's a stretch of silence, the only sound our shoes scuffing against the cement as we walk. Mike pauses and then glances at the side of my face. "By the way...," he says. "Sorry."

Now I'm looking at the side of his face. "What?"

"I'm sorry. For lying and tricking you into going to Oliver's." He looks ashamed. "I was just thinking about when my dad pulled out the gun. What if he took a shot? What if you got hit? It would have been my fault."

I'm quiet. That really would have been a terrible thing.

And no one in my family would have known what I was even doing there if it ended that way. "Well, it's a good thing nothing happened," I say. I glance at Mike's ankle and the scrapes on the palms of my hands. "Sort of."

"Yeah. Anyway." Mike tosses me a grin. "I'll make it up to you. I promised you I'd help you get to your store and I'm gonna keep that promise. I'll convince Hae Dang to take us there once we meet him at the noraebang."

"Thanks," I say, smiling back.

I feel lighter than I have all night. Everything's been going wrong, but it looks like things are finally headed in the right direction. My steps feel more hopeful, almost like I'm floating. Even the gun doesn't feel so heavy in my backpack anymore.

"By the way, what do you need to go to your store for?" Mike asks.

Suddenly, some of that light, floating feeling goes away.

I still haven't told Mike about the gun. What would he say? Would he understand? Or would he think it's too much, even for him? Would he get mad that I've been keeping a secret from him this whole night, especially after he just said sorry for his own secret? But everyone has secrets, don't they? Just because one person shares theirs doesn't mean everyone has to.

Just tell him, I think. *What are you scared of? You're just doing what you need to do. This is the right thing.*

But when I open my mouth, what I hear myself say is:

"Just some family stuff."

"What family stuff?"

"I can't really talk about it."

"Why not?"

I sigh, the grateful feeling I had for Mike just a second ago quickly disappearing. "I just can't."

"Come on, dude, we're friends," Mike says. "You can tell me. You told me when your parents had to sell their last store because it wasn't doing well. Remember? Didn't it go bankrupt? Wait. Does it have something to do with that?"

"Mike, stop asking!" I shout. I'm not just annoyed now, I'm angry. "How come you can never take a hint?"

He looks surprised, and then embarrassed. "Sorry. I was just curious." He's quiet for a bit and then he adds, "I always thought your dad was cool. Whatever reason you're going to see him, I hope he's okay."

This makes me pause to look at him. "Cool?"

I never really thought of Appa as cool before. When I think of Appa, I think of his furrowed brow and the way he frowns. Lately, it seems like he frowns more than he smiles. Was it always like that? It feels like it.

"Yeah," Mike says, grinning again. "You know when we all go to the church kitchen after service to eat? And like, all the other adults are talking and hanging out, and your dad will just be sitting there, quietly eating his bibimbap. But then every once in a while, he'll make eye contact with one of the kids and wave them over and give them a stick of gum. Remember? That was cool of him. We were always trying to get him to look at us so we could get some gum. It's been a while since he's done that, but man, I don't know what it is—free gum just tastes better."

At first, I don't remember that at all, and then I do.

Appa used to always have yellow packets of Juicy Fruit in his pockets that he'd share with the kids at church. He would chew a lot of gum whenever he was trying to quit smoking.

No matter how many he gave away, though, he always saved a piece for me and Sarah for the car ride home. The two of us would pile into the back seat and he would hand us each a stick of gum as he pulled out of the parking lot.

Sometimes while he was driving, he'd hold out his hand to us in the back seat and say, "Give me your hand."

I'd stick my palm in his and he'd bite my hand, light and playful, just enough to make me laugh. "You okay?" he'd say, and I'd grin and nod.

I forgot about those car rides. I forgot about the gum.

I hope he's okay, I think. I grip my backpack straps tight. *He has to be.*

"Earth to Jordan." Mike waves a hand in front of my face. "We need to cross the street."

I didn't even realize it, but we're back on Vermont, standing at a crosswalk. Even more stores are closed now, whether it's late or it's because of the state of emergency, I'm not sure. We cross the road and keep on walking, and I can feel my heart pounding in my chest. It looks like the protests and fires haven't reached here yet. But will they? Mike keeps looking over his shoulder and I wonder if he's thinking the same thing, like he's just waiting for the smoke to catch up to us. I can't shake the feeling that at any turn we could see the city going up in flames.

I try not to think about it, try to keep my eyes on all the rectangular signs we pass by instead.

Quality Dry Cleaning
21 Minute Photo
Open 24 Hours

But when I hear the sirens, I can't help but whirl around, fear trapped in my throat.

Three police cars whiz down the street and I think two things at once.

The first is, *the riots.* I can almost hear the looters, the sound of smashing glass and roaring fires, TVs and furniture being carried on people's backs as they run through the streets, shouting and shouting, breaking everything standing in their way.

The second is, *Or is it me they're coming for?*

But the police cars don't stop, not for me or any sign of rioting. Instead, they keep going, leaving Koreatown, heading north. The sound of looters was just all in my head.

I don't realize I'm still staring after the police cars, not moving, until Mike shakes my arm. "Jordan? C'mon. Silver Star is right there." He gives me a funny look. "You okay?"

"Yeah." I take a deep breath and start walking again. "I'm good."

As we get closer to Silver Star, I see a car parked in front of the karaoke place. But it's not Hae Dang's.

It's a way-too-familiar-looking Hyundai Excel.

The driver's door opens and someone steps out.

Sarah.

CHAPTER NINE

There was a time when Sarah was my favorite person. When I would sit by the classroom window and watch the clock, waiting for the minutes to go by until I would see her jogging across the playground to pick me up. She was the one who held my hand when we crossed the street, the one who listened to me talk about my day, who would let me stop and play on the way home and push me on the swings until her arms ached. Umma always says that when we first moved to America, I wouldn't go anywhere unless Sarah was there too because she was the one I knew the best.

But that was then and this is now and I can't think of anyone else I'd rather see less.

"Jordan! Thank God!"

Sarah runs toward me and suddenly I feel like my feet have grown tree roots, digging deep into the cement, so deep that I don't move—can't move—as she pulls me into a hug.

"I'm so glad you're okay," she says, relieved.

She lets go and starts checking my face and my arms. "Are you okay? You're not hurt, right? Oh my God, what happened to your hands?" Her voice gets frantic now and her worry turns into anger. "I can't believe you did this, Jordan. Are you completely out of your mind? What have you been doing out here? You know what, I don't even want to know. Actually, no, tell me everything."

I snap out of it, pulling up my imaginary tree roots and stepping away. "Sarah, I'm fine. What are you doing here? How did you find me? Does Umma know?"

My mind is going so fast, all my questions pour out at once.

She's not listening, though. She's looking at Mike now, who's just as confused as me, his eyes going back and forth between me and Sarah, his face a big question mark.

"You're not Hae Dang," he says.

Well, obviously, Mike! I want to shout.

"Come on," Sarah says, reaching for Mike. She takes his arm in one hand, mine in the other, and starts steering us toward the car, seething mad. "We have to get home. We shouldn't be out here."

I tug my arm out of her grasp and step back again. She sighs, letting go of Mike to put her hands on her hips. Her eyes flash.

"Jordan, seriously? You're going to make this difficult?"

"I said, what are you doing here? How did you find me?" I repeat. I'm not just confused now. I'm angry. Annoyed.

Sarah wasn't part of the plan.

"I'll explain in the car—" she starts.

I shake my head and plant my feet like tree roots again, only this time on purpose. I'm not going anywhere with her.

"Fine." Now she's the one who looks annoyed. "I knocked on your door to see if you needed help with your homework. When you didn't answer, I opened the door and saw that you were gone. I completely freaked out."

"Did you—" I can barely talk, I'm so shaken. "Did you tell Umma?"

She presses her lips together, shakes her head. Her usually perfect hair is falling out of her ponytail. "No. Umma doesn't know you're gone, and she doesn't know I left either. Yet. She's probably figured it out by now with both of us missing. Anyway, I called Hae Dang to see if he might know where you are. You were talking on the phone with Mike earlier so I thought—"

"Hae Dang told you where I was?" I look at Mike and repeat, "Hae Dang told her."

"How'd he tell her?" Mike says.

"If you would stop interrupting me!" Sarah cries. She keeps going, talking fast, her eyes darting around the street like she's keeping watch at the same time. "Hae Dang didn't know. He said he dropped you off at Oliver's, but when he came back to pick you up, you were both gone. He said he was driving around for a while, trying to find you, and then he decided to go back home so if you called, he'd be right by the phone."

"But it was you that called instead," I say.

"Right. And I told him to call me back right away if he heard from you. And he did. He said Mike sent him a message on his pager telling him to meet you at Silver Star Karaoke and I told him I would go pick you up."

"Why?" I say, when what I really mean is *Why are you getting in the way? Why do you always have to ruin everything?*

"You think I'm going to trust Hae Dang to pick you up when he's the one who got you into this mess in the first place?" she says in disbelief. "No. No way."

"Well, it wasn't exactly Hae Dang's fault," Mike says hesitantly. "Going to Oliver's was my idea."

Sarah shakes her head, tightening her ponytail, trying to get it back under control. "Doesn't matter whose idea it was. Hae Dang is older than you. He should have been responsible enough not to leave you alone."

"Well, maybe he's not the kind of older sibling who always has to keep an eye on their younger brother," I snap. "Not everyone wants to be watched over all the time, Sarah."

Her mouth falls open. "What's that supposed to mean?"

"Forget it."

"No, really. What do you mean? I snuck out of the

house without Umma knowing to come and pick you up in the middle of the night during a *state of emergency* when the whole city is bursting into flames. Because why?" Her voice is rising now, louder than I've ever heard it, and her face is getting redder by the second. "Because you decided to sneak out for God knows what reason, and if anything happened to you, I'd never forgive myself. Not to mention, Umma and Appa would kill me. It's my job to take care of you. My job to make sure you're okay. So yeah, you better believe I'm keeping watch over you. And you should thank me for it!"

"I never asked you to!" I shout back, not caring that Mike is standing right there, not caring if anyone passing us on the street can hear, not caring if all of Los Angeles shakes with my yells. "I never asked you to do anything. I can take care of this on my own. I don't need your rescuing!"

"And what exactly are you trying to take care of?" Sarah says. Her hair is getting so messy, she gives up on her ponytail altogether, tugging the elastic out and slipping it around her wrist with an angry *snap!* "You're just out here, hanging out with Mike."

"Actually, he's been trying to get to your family's store," Mike says before I can reply. He gives me a knowing nod like he thinks he's helping.

My stomach sinks.

"The store?" Sarah blinks. "Why?"

"Family stuff," Mike says.

She stares at him. And then she stares at me.

"What family stuff?" she says.

"You don't need to know about it," I say. All my guards are up. I feel like I'm in a boxing ring, gloves up to my face. I didn't even want to tell Mike about the gun. There's no way I'm telling Sarah about it.

"You think I don't need to know about our family stuff?"

"Just leave me alone, Sarah!" I yell. I don't want to talk about this anymore.

Mike just stands there, looking full of regrets. I know that look. The *I shouldn't have said anything* look. But I'm not mad at Mike. He probably thought he was saying the right thing, that maybe Sarah could even drive us to the store.

But I can't go with Sarah. I was supposed to prove that *I* can do this, not *I can do this with Sarah's help.* I don't need her help. More than that, I don't want it.

Sarah lets out a frustrated noise, dragging her hands down her face. "God. Please, Jordan. You have no idea how bad things are getting out here."

"Actually, I do," I say, thinking about the news.

"No! You don't! I overheard Umma on the phone talking with one of her friends and it sounds like some of the looters are specifically targeting Korean-owned stores. They heard there were already a couple that were burned down in South Central. If Umma and her friend are right, there's no telling when they'll start moving up to Koreatown."

My whole body goes still. "Targeting Korean stores? Why?"

Sarah looks away, going quieter now. "It could be because they're mad about the light sentence Soon Ja Du got after killing Latasha Harlins. You remember how the news about the state court of appeal just came out last week."

"But—that—what about our store? Have you heard from him? Have you tried calling?"

She presses her lips together, shakes her head. "We haven't heard from him yet. And our calls haven't been going through. But we also haven't heard anything about the riots moving that far north yet. Umma hasn't turned the news off since dinner. If anything were to happen in that area, she'd know it."

My head is spinning, my heart pounding. Somewhere in the back of my mind, I realize that I'm wasting time. If I want to get to Appa and make sure he's okay, the fastest thing to do at this point would be to get into Sarah's car and convince her to take us to the store. It would be quick if we all went together.

But the front of my mind is louder. The stubborn part, the part that's angry that she's here at all, the part that's saying *Let me do this my own way.*

"Come on," Sarah says. She walks to the car, opens the back door. "Let's just get somewhere safer. Please?"

I don't move.

"Jordan! Can you not be such a brat about this? I'm trying to save us!" she cries, losing her patience.

If I was more like Sarah, I would take her invitation

and get into the car. I would be calm, think straight, act reasonable.

But I'm not Sarah.

I'm Jordan.

So here's what I do instead.

I grab Mike's arm and I run.

CHAPTER TEN

I know it's a bad idea to run away the second I do it. I count all the reasons why in my head.

Number one: Mike's ankle is sprained. He was just able to walk and now I'm making him run. He can't even use his branch cane, which he's still holding in his hand, for support.

Number two: Sarah swears—it's maybe the first time I've ever heard her swear in my life—and moves to get into her car. She's on wheels. We're on foot. Do I really think we can outrun her?

Number three: Where am I even going?

I don't know. All I know is that I need to get to Appa,

and Sarah's in my way. That there's something like fire in my veins, angry and hot, pushing me in the opposite direction from her. I duck down a side street, then another, cutting through alleyways to try to lose her. The gun in my backpack feels like it's getting bigger by the minute, weighing me down, threatening to swallow me whole. I need to protect it because Appa needs it to protect him. But I can't let Sarah see it. She won't understand. I need to do this on my own.

"Jordan," Mike pants. "I think I'm going to throw up."

I'm still running, my hand tight around Mike's arm. I slow down, let go. Mike bends over, hands against his legs, but he doesn't throw up. He's just breathing heavy. I can almost see his ankle throbbing from here.

We're on a more residential street now. I keep one eye out for Sarah. We bought some time, but she saw which way we were going and she knows we won't be able to move far. She'll show up sooner rather than later. We've got to get out of here, fast.

My eyes fall on a man across the street, rearranging something in the back of his dark green pickup truck. He's a big, stocky guy wearing a tan work shirt, painter's pants, and a Lakers cap. *He's my only hope*, I think. I turn to Mike.

"One last run," I say. "I promise."

Mike groans but straightens up anyway. This time I help him, putting his arm around my shoulders again. We race across the street.

"Sir!" I yell at the man.

He startles, looking up from his truck. The back is filled to the brim with gardening supplies: rakes, shovels, buckets, a long, tangled hose. It looks like he was right in the middle of flipping over a wheelbarrow from the way one of the wheels is slowly spinning in the air.

"Could we get a ride?" I ask, breathless. "My friend. He needs help."

I know I'm using Mike as an excuse but it's hard to say no to two kids when one of the kids is hurt.

The man's face fills with worry. Seeing him up close, I'd guess he's just a bit younger than Appa. "You two out here alone?" he asks, looking over our shoulders. He has a slight accent, maybe Mexican, and wrinkles that look like ocean waves across his forehead.

"We don't live far from here," I say. The lie comes easy. "We're on our way home and my friend got hurt. We're just a few blocks away. Like half a mile south?"

Mike doesn't even have to act this time. The man hesitates for a second and then nods, dusting the wheelbarrow dirt from his hands, and heads for the driver's seat. "All right, hop in. Young kids like you shouldn't be out so late alone, especially on a night like this. But I have to warn you ... it's pretty crowded in here."

My heart is pounding as I open the passenger door, ushering Mike in. The man wasn't kidding when he said it was crowded. There's one bench seat in the front and, other than the driver's part, it's completely packed with bags of fertilizer and empty watering cans. I squeeze into the middle, my face nearly right up against the radio dial, and Mike slides in next to me, trying not to bang his ankle against anything. His branch won't fit inside with us so he leaves it out on the sidewalk, giving it a gentle pat. "You did well."

I throw a quick glance behind my shoulder and my heart nearly stops. Sarah's car is turning onto the street. Shoot. Shoot shoot shoot.

"Sir, we're ready to go!" I nearly shout.

"You able to get your seat belts on?" he asks, turning the ignition.

"We're good," I say, looking over my shoulder again. Sarah is close enough now that I can just make out her face through the windshield. She sees me and her eyes widen in disbelief. Her mouth drops open and she rolls down her window, starts to shout, "Don't you dare—!" but I don't hear the rest because the man steps on the gas, peeling away.

I let myself breathe, just a bit.

"I'm Luis, by the way," the man says.

"Nice to meet you, sir," I say. "I'm Jordan. This is Mike."

"Sorry about all the fertilizer," he says. "It was a big supply run day and I haven't had a chance to unload."

"It's a little tight," Mike says. He's got his foot propped up on top of the watering can, his hands relaxed behind his head. "But I'm okay."

Me? I'm sitting right on the edge of the seat, heavy bags of fertilizer pressed right up against my back. I wriggle my backpack off and put it down at my feet to give me more space. It's not a huge difference but at least my nose isn't so close to the dashboard anymore.

"Thanks for giving us a ride," I say. We're back on Vermont again. I keep my eyes on the rearview mirror. Sarah's behind us, just a couple of cars back, following us.

"Sure," Luis says. He looks tired, like this isn't the first time he's had to pick up random hitchhikers on his way home. "You're lucky I'm even out this late. One of my workers left his wallet at a client's house and I live the closest, so I said I'd pick it up. I swear, that guy would lose his head if it wasn't attached." He fiddles with the radio, switching from playing Spanish music to Spanish news. "Hope you don't mind. I've been waiting for a news update. Now, where am I going?"

Mike looks at me and it takes me a second to realize Luis is talking to us. Where *are* we going?

"Uh, take a left here," I say.

He takes a left.

"Another left," I say. "Now a right. Keep going. Another right. Right. Left. Left. Right."

I'm totally making this up as we go. I keep my eyes on the mirror the whole time, praying that we're getting Sarah off our tail. She falls behind another car, then another, until I can't see her anymore.

I let myself breathe even more.

Luis makes a humming sound of disapproval at something the radio host says. "Terrible night tonight," he murmurs, almost to himself.

"Are there any news updates on the riots?" I ask, sitting up straighter. Or as straight as I possibly can with all the fertilizer bags around me.

"According to the radio, we're not seeing a lot of police support in the riot zones," Luis says. "And some of the phone lines are down."

The phone lines? Could that be why we haven't heard from Appa yet? I think of the police cars I saw earlier, whizzing in the opposite direction of South Central, out of Koreatown, and the footage from earlier tonight where the stores were being looted with no help in sight. *Please let him be okay*, I think.

"A few exit ramps off the 110 Freeway have been shut down so drivers don't wander into the violence as well." Luis shakes his head and says again, "Terrible night tonight. You know it is my daughter's fifth birthday today?"

"Is it?" I think of Mr. Gary's Super Deluxe Burger tradition for special occasions.

"Yes. We got her an ice cream cake, so for her, it is a great day. Funny how that is, isn't it? She wished that every day could be her birthday, but I sure hope no other day will be like this one."

"I love ice cream cake," Mike says. He thinks for a moment. "I would have wished for another turtle."

I raise my eyebrows. "What do you need another one for?"

"I don't know. Wizard is getting old."

Luis peers worriedly out the window. "Where did you say you live again?" he asks. "Because we're almost in South Central now and I won't be going too much more south from here. It's not safe."

South Central? I sit up straighter, looking out the window at the street signs. It's Arlington—we're definitely closer to the store now. I think it's just a few more blocks down and then to the right from there.

My heart lifts.

We've nearly made it.

The streets around here are still pretty quiet, and by that, I mean no looters as far as I can tell. Yet. In the distance, I see clouds of smoke billowing into the air. My throat gets tighter, seeing them in person, even from far away. How much longer until the fires get closer?

"Whoa," Mike says, seeing the smoke too.

"Sir, we'll get out here," I say to Luis. "It's not too far. It's just a couple of blocks away."

"No, no. I can take you to your door. I wouldn't feel right about letting you kids walk the rest of the way home. Just look at that smoke!"

I chew my lip. The thing is, I can't remember the exact address of the store. And even if I did, I can't tell Luis to drop us off there. "This doesn't look like a home," he'd say. The lie that we lived close might have come easy, but it doesn't feel so easy to keep it going. If he's not going to drop us off here, how willing would he be to leave us at some random store? I could say we're meeting my dad there, but what if Appa's not even there? And besides, that's not what I told Luis at first. I can't just change my story.

"Just keep going straight," I say.

But Luis is still looking worriedly at the smoke. "You know what? I'm going to go around this." He signals left, heading in the exact opposite direction of the store. "Tell me the address. We'll find a safe route to get you boys home."

Oh man. My mind is whirring fast. "Actually, it's probably more than a couple of blocks. We'll have to go further south, so if you don't want to drive there, we'll just get out here. It's really no problem." I'm rambling. I'm so nervous I'm starting to sweat.

Luis looks at me out of the corner of his eye, frowning. "Do you not know exactly where you live? What's your address?" he asks.

"Um... It's..."

My mind totally blanks. I have no idea what to say.

Now Luis looks suspicious. "What did you two say you were doing out again?"

I rack my brain. *Come on, Jordan. Say something. Anything!* "Playing Nintendo at a friend's house," I blurt out.

"His name is Ben," Mike adds.

Luis's frown deepens like he's not sure whether to believe us or not. "All right. Well, what's your address?" he asks again.

I glance over at Mike. He mouths, *What now?*

The truck starts to slow down as we approach a red light. I'm panicking real bad. All I can think about is how we need to get out of this truck *now*.

I hold up three fingers to Mike. *Jump*, I mouth back.

Two fingers.

The truck rolls to a stop.

One.

Mike throws open the door. Luis yells, "What the——?" as we jump out of the truck, slamming the door shut behind us and running as fast as we can, cars honking behind us.

We jump onto the sidewalk and keep on running. I look behind me only once to see that the light's turned green. The car behind Luis keeps honking until eventually the truck rolls away, disappearing down the street.

My steps slow down. We turn into the empty parking lot of a closed BBQ joint, collapsing on the concrete. Mike and I look at each other, breathing hard, finally able to really catch our breath.

"You're a liar," Mike says. He lies down on his back, his chest rising and falling.

"I know," I say. "I just didn't know what else to tell him. I should have given him a fake home address nearby or something!"

"Not to Luis," Mike says. "To me. You promised no more running." He laughs loud, palms pressed against his stomach. "Liar."

"Sorry," I say. I mean it too. "You might need that ankle transplant after all."

He laughs again and then I'm laughing too, and suddenly, I can't stop laughing. I lie down on my back, right there in the parking lot, opposite Mike, the soles of our sneakers leaning against each other as we laugh and laugh and laugh. Little teardrops form at the corners of my eyes, I'm laughing so hard.

"Wait till I tell Hae Dang about this," Mike says.

"Yeah." I sit up, wiping at my eyes. The adrenaline from jumping out of the truck dies down a bit. I know we can't sit here forever. We should get a move on. I feel like I've been refilled with energy now that we're so close to the store. So close to what I've been trying to do this whole night.

So close to . . .

I freeze suddenly, my body going still.

"Jordan?" Mike says, sitting up.

The gun.

I left the gun in the truck.

CHAPTER ELEVEN

"What's wrong?" Mike asks.

I can't speak. It feels like my whole body has turned to ice. No, fire. I'm hot and cold at the same time, shaking, thinking, *No no no it can't be I can't have left it in the truck there's no way* . . .

But it's true.

I did.

"The gun," I finally manage to say. My voice doesn't sound like my voice. It sounds like a stranger. I feel almost like I've floated out of my body and I'm watching myself, sitting in the parking lot, all the blood draining from my face.

"Huh?" Mike frowns. "What gun?"

"My backpack," I say. "The gun was there."

He shakes his head. "Dude. Can you talk in real sentences? I have no idea what you're saying."

"The gun was inside my backpack!" I yell, exploding.

I don't feel like I'm floating anymore. I feel like the opposite now. Like I've collided with my own body and now I'm bruised all over. I can't think straight. How did this happen? How?

Mike stares. "There was a gun in your backpack?"

"It was my dad's. I wanted to bring it to him. For protection."

I'm on my feet now, pacing back and forth. I can't believe I did this. I can't believe I lost Appa's gun.

"Whoa," Mike says, standing to join me. "Was that the family stuff you were talking about? You wanted to bring a gun to your dad?" His eyes go huge. "I can't believe you had a gun on you this whole time and you didn't tell me. And after you got so mad that I lied about going to Ben's!"

"It's not the same thing," I say.

"How's it different?"

"I don't know, but it's not the same!"

"Okay, so you had the gun and then what? You lost it in the truck?" He laughs. "Man, Jordan, that's—"

I act before I can think. I whirl around and push Mike hard in the chest.

"Jordan!" he yells, stumbling backward.

"It's not funny," I say, breathing hard.

"I never said it was!"

"You laughed."

"Okay, well, yeah, maybe it's kind of funny if you really think about it—"

I push him again. I know I'm overreacting, but I can't stop myself. I've had enough of his comments, can't stand the way he's not seeing how serious this is, can't stand myself for getting into this whole mess in the first place. This time, when he catches his balance, he turns to me, angry, and pushes me back.

"Stop doing that!" he yells.

Realization slowly sinks in as I stare at Mike. His tall hair, his sweaty face, his too-big T-shirt that's probably one of Hae Dang's hand-me-downs. This is all *his* fault.

"This is because of you," I say.

"What are you talking about?"

I'm seething now, stepping forward, pushing him again. "This is because you made me go to Oliver's with you. If you had just let me go to my family's store in the first place, then none of this would have happened!"

"How is that my fault? Hae Dang said he wouldn't drive you, remember? I was the one who said I'd try to convince him to change his mind afterward!" he shouts, pushing me back.

Somewhere in the back of my mind, and not even very far back, I know that what Mike is saying is true. But right now, I'm so mad, I don't care.

"You're a liar," I say. "You should have told me about the money from the start. I would have never gone with you if I knew."

"If I'm a liar, so are you," he says, scowling. "You should have told *me* about the gun from the start. Huh? Did you ever think about that?" He shakes his head. "You're selfish, Jordan. You're only thinking about yourself."

His words set me off. My fist goes flying into his face. I'm out of control. Even in this state, I can't help but think of what Mr. Gary said. How the uprisings of tonight are from years of unheard anger, how people are setting the city on fire not because they love to see it burn but because they're in pain. And I know it's not at all the same, what I'm going through now, but I think I get it more than I did before. The feeling of being so mad you can't help yourself. Mike touches the corner of his lip, brings his fingers back bloody. He stares at me in disbelief.

"You're serious?" he says. "Fine."

He punches me back, square in the nose. I reel backward, pain splitting my head. My ears pound. And then I'm punching him again. We're both hitting and shouting and pushing, catching each other in the eyes, the chest, the side of our ears, noses bleeding, heads spinning. I've never been in a fight before. All the adrenaline from jumping out of the truck comes roaring back ten times stronger than before and for a second, I forget about the gun and how I let it go. As long as I'm fighting, I'm not thinking about the gun. All I'm thinking about is dodging Mike's fists, getting even, ignoring the fear pressing against my lungs as I aim my next swing. I keep going until Mike bites me in the arm and I have to shake him off, yelling, stumbling back.

We stare at each other, breathing hard. His hair is messed up, hanging in his eyes. No amount of gel can save him now. I don't know how I look, but I know it's probably just as bad.

With our fists down, the truth sinks into me again.

I lost Appa's gun. And the truck it's in is long gone now.

"My parents were right," I say. "I never should have hung out with you. You're a troublemaker."

Mike laughs again and gives me that wide crocodile grin of his. "That's really funny coming from you. If I'm a troublemaker, you are too. You act like you're so much better, but you're not so different."

"At least I don't steal from my own family."

"Don't you? Were you allowed to take your dad's gun?"

My chest is tight. I turn away and start walking, the adrenaline still pulsing through me. My hands are shaking. My whole body is.

"Where are you going?" he shouts.

I don't stop to answer. Instead, I start running, knowing he won't be able to chase me.

CHAPTER TWELVE

I know I'm close to our store.

The buildings around me are familiar. There's that sandwich shop with the bright orange sign on the door advertising the best mustard in town, and that hair salon two doors down with the row of stuffed bears sitting along the window ledge inside, next to a pile of crinkled old magazines that never change.

I'm lucky. The riot still hasn't touched this part of South Central yet. There are no looters, no fires. But the sky is getting even smokier, and I don't know if it's my imagination, but I can almost smell the ashes in the air.

If I go just a few blocks down the street, I'll be at our store. But how can I go now?

I sit down on the steps of the sandwich shop. It's closed, boarded up, just like what Appa went to our store to do. I wonder if he made it. If he ever ended up calling home. I could go see for myself.

But what will I say when I see him?

Hi, Appa. I came all this way to give you your gun so you can protect yourself.

But then I lost it.

How am I supposed to face him like this?

Without Mike, everything feels way too quiet around me. I can't believe I hit him like that. I just really couldn't control myself. And now...

I'm all alone.

I put my hands in my pockets and remember the crumpled photographs. I pull them out. There's me and Appa with his poetry book, and three other pictures.

One of me and Sarah sitting on a skateboard together, Sarah in the back with her arms tight around me, both of us smiling.

A blurry one of Harabeoji on the edge of the couch, putting on his slippers.

And one last one, of Umma and Appa standing in front of their store the day it opened.

Not the liquor store we have now, the one I'm just a few blocks away from, but the convenience store they had before that. The one that failed.

That was about a year and a half ago. Umma and Appa both worked hard, but the thing is, Appa was never very good at it. Not the way Umma was. She was good at the business side and good at the dealing-with-people side too. Appa would sometimes get so lost in a book during his break that he would forget to go back to the cash register.

"You are always dreaming," I heard Umma say to him once.

"Is that so bad?" he answered.

"It is when I need you here working. I can't do this alone."

He tried, they both did, but eventually they had to close the store and sell it. Sarah and I didn't know all the reasons why. Umma and Appa never told us much about it, just said they would be doing some different things for a bit. For a while, Umma worked at a dry cleaner's owned by a woman from church, and Appa did a bunch of odd jobs like house painting. And then the liquor store came along.

A couple of my parents' friends were looking to sell their store and they gave Umma and Appa the first go at it. "Praise God for this second chance!" Umma said.

Since they got the liquor store, they've been working harder than ever. I never saw much of them to begin with, but now it feels like I really never do. Appa especially started changing a lot with the new store. He got more angry more often. And he stopped reading poetry.

Eventually, it all led up to the Big Fight.

Now I'm thinking about everything I've been trying not to think about. It comes in one great wave, and suddenly, I'm drowning in it.

>>>>

The Big Fight with Appa happened a few weeks ago. Almost a month now.

It was a Sunday.

We got to church late that day, Umma, Appa, Sarah, and

me. Harabeoji doesn't go with us. He says it's because he doesn't believe in God, but I think it might also be because he likes having a day where he has the whole apartment to himself.

Umma and Appa went into the main sanctuary for the adult service, Sarah to the attic for the teen group, and me to the rec room where the middle school kids meet. At least, I was headed there. I was just about to go in when Mike called my name from down the hall.

"I was waiting for you!" he said. "I want to show you something."

He zipped open his backpack. I looked inside to see a can of red spray paint.

"Where'd you get that?" I asked.

"I got it off a hyung I know," he said, grinning. "He's awesome and really into writing graffiti. It's almost empty, but I think there's enough paint in it to write something. Want to come along?"

"Now?" I looked toward the rec room.

"Come on. It'll be fun! Just come with me," he said.

I hesitated. But I was too curious to say no.

We snuck out one of the back doors. I was thinking

maybe we'd find a big rock to spray-paint or something like that, but Mike stopped at the back wall of the church, giving it a long hard look.

"I think this is it," he said.

"This? You mean the church building?"

"It's the perfect place, don't you think?" He dropped his backpack on the ground and took out the can of spray paint, shaking it. "What do you think my name should be? I've never done this before, but I've always wanted to try."

"We can't do this here," I said, looking around to see if anyone was watching. No one was, but I still felt an uneasy feeling creep into my stomach. "That's vandalizing."

"What if I just did a really small thing, on the corner over there?" He pointed to the side of the wall where the brown paint was already chipping. "They have to repaint that section anyway."

I chewed my lip. This was a bad idea. "I don't know..."

But he was already running with it, way too excited. "I was thinking WIZZ. For my name. You know, in honor of my turtle."

He popped the top off the can and started painting on the wall with a *hissss*. I watched, practically holding my breath, as he began writing WIZZ. He was careful about it, spelling each letter out real slow in a blocky, squarish style. The way he was writing it, it wasn't totally clear what he was spelling unless you knew what to look for. It actually looked kind of fun.

"What do you think?" he asked.

"Not bad," I said, still nervous. "But we should probably go now."

He stepped aside, holding out the can. "Want to give it a shot? You can borrow my name if you want."

I glanced over my shoulder again. The coast was clear. I knew I shouldn't do it, but I did want to try. Just a little bit. And with Mike's writing already on the wall, the church would definitely have to repaint it now. It would be gone before we knew it.

Okay. Just one small word. Palms sweaty, I took the can from Mike and stepped toward the wall, starting on the *W*. My hand shook, making the paint come out wobbly. I'd barely had time to finish the letter when I heard the crunch of footsteps behind me and a voice shouting, "Ya! Jordan! What are you doing?"

The can dropped from my hand. I whirled around and

saw Appa standing there, a look of disbelief on his face. His hands were on his hips, a cigarette between two fingers.

Oh no.

No no no.

This has got to be the worst timing for his smoke break ever.

"Uh, Mr. Park, I can explain—" Mike started.

But Appa wasn't having it. He strode forward and took me by the arm, dragging me away from Mike. He dropped the cigarette on the ground, crushing it with his shoe before taking me back into the church building.

"Appa, I'm sorry," I blurted out.

"We'll talk about this later." He took me into the sanctuary, where all the adults were sitting. Heads turned to look at us, but Appa didn't acknowledge any of them. He put me in the pew next to Umma and sat on my other side without a word. Umma glanced at me in confusion and then at Appa. "Weh?" she mouthed.

But Appa didn't answer why. Instead, he just stared straight ahead at the pastor, his jaw set tight.

The ride home that day was quiet and tense. Even Sarah could tell that something had happened. She took one look at Appa and then at me and then clamped her mouth shut the whole way home. Umma tried to make small talk, but even she eventually faded off to silence.

As soon as we got home, though, the cold shoulder was over. Appa called me into the kitchen. "Everyone else out," he said.

At that moment, I wished we had stayed in the silence a little longer.

I sat down across from him at the kitchen table and stared down at my hands.

"Look at me," he said.

I did.

"What is wrong with you?"

I winced. "It was only a little bit of the wall. Mike said they'd have to paint over it anyway."

"Is that supposed to make it better? I don't know what's gotten into you lately, Jordan. The graffiti. The grades."

My stomach sank. I wasn't expecting the grades to come up. Truth was, I was having a hard time in school since sixth grade started. School wasn't always hard. For a long time, it was even kind of fun, the place where I got to see my friends and get out of the house. But lately I was struggling, and home was feeling smaller than usual. Anytime Umma and Appa weren't working, they were there, fighting, stressing, talking in low voices about how they couldn't let this business fail, they just couldn't. Sometimes the low voices got loud, but whenever I would poke my head in, Umma would wave me away. "Geokjeonghajima," she said.

Don't worry. Always don't worry.

After that was the history test. A big red D at the top of my paper.

I crumpled it, dropped it in my backpack.

The tests kept piling up like snowballs in my bag. And the thing was, I couldn't explain it, even if I wanted to. I didn't know how to explain that school was hard for me. That ever since Sarah got busier with volleyball and all her other clubs, I would come home after school and just watch TV with Harabeoji because it was easier than trying to do anything else. That by the time Umma and Appa came home from work and asked me if I did my homework, it was also easier to lie and say *Yes of course* because they already looked so tired, I didn't want to add any more worry onto their shoulders. That whenever I did try to sit down to study, all I could see was their stressed faces, full of things they wouldn't tell me about.

Don't worry, Umma would say, trying to protect me from their world where there wasn't enough money.

Don't worry, I would say back, trying to protect them from my world where there wasn't enough focus.

Geokjeonghajima. Back and forth, just like that, protecting each other from our worlds until we were living on two totally different planets.

"How'd you find out?" I asked.

"Your teacher left us a message. Said they were worried about you."

That was news to me. "You didn't say anything."

"I thought you would eventually tell me yourself, but I guess I expected too much from you," Appa said, shaking his head. "I don't understand it, Jordan. You're just throwing your whole life away already."

"I'm not—"

"You're being lazy. Would it hurt you so much to try even a little bit in school? Look at how well Sarah does. Why can't you be more like your sister?"

"I don't—"

"And the graffiti! Now you're going around vandalizing church property? I don't understand when you became such a bad kid."

"You're not listening to me!" I shouted. It was the first time I'd ever shouted at my dad. He looked shocked. And then he looked mad.

"Why should I listen to you? You're selfish. Selfish! You think of no one but yourself. Do you know how much we've sacrificed for you?"

He was yelling too now, his voice shaking the walls. "We came to this country for *you*. We break our backs working all day and all night for *you*. So you can have a better life and have all the opportunities in the world. But you don't even care! You don't see your sister doing this kind of thing!"

That really pushed me over the edge. All I could see was red-hot anger. "If you think Sarah's so great, you should have just had her, then! Why'd you go and have a second kid, huh? Sounds like your life would have been just perfect if you only had Sarah to worry about."

"Maybe it would have been," he said.

I stared at him in disbelief, and he looked away, pressing his lips together.

"Well, I wish you had just left me behind in Korea," I said. My hands were clenched tight into fists, my nails digging into my palms. "Maybe I could have been adopted into a new family or something. Anyone would have been better than you."

I shoved my chair back and got up from the table.

"Ya! Where are you going? Did I say you could leave?" Appa said.

I wanted to run far, far away, but his voice rooted me to the spot. I stood there shaking and I could feel tears start to prick my eyes.

Appa put his head in his hands, his shoulders rising and falling like he was taking deep breaths to try to calm himself down. When he lifted his head again, his face was grim. "You are not to hang out with Mike anymore. Understood? That kid causes trouble wherever he goes."

I didn't say anything. I just glared at him.

"Jordan? Answer me when I'm talking to you."

Still silence.

"You're really going to be like this, huh?" He shook his

head, brow furrowed in frustration. "You are my biggest disappointment."

"Yeah, well, maybe you're mine too. All this talk about doing everything for me and you couldn't even keep our last store open. Why'd we even come here if you can't do that?"

I could see the change in his face, this look like I had somehow betrayed him. I regretted it as soon as I said it.

"What am I going to do with you?" he said. His voice was flat now, his eyes dead.

I ran out of the kitchen and he didn't try to stop me. I went into my room, slamming the door shut, grabbing my backpack, and turning it upside down. Balls of paper fell out like an avalanche. All the failed tests I'd been hiding. I grabbed them in handfuls, ripping them to shreds, turning them into little pieces of snow until my fingers were covered in paper cuts and the floor was covered in Appa's disappointment.

Here's what I didn't tell Appa.

I didn't tell him that I was sorry, when I was.

I didn't tell him that I cared, when I did.

I didn't tell him that after the Big Fight, I started

cheating on tests to try to get my grades up fast and make things better between us.

It didn't make things better.

I got suspended instead. And now I've lost his gun.

I think I've just proven for good that Appa was right.

I am the biggest disappointment.

CHAPTER THIRTEEN

There's nothing left to do now but to face Appa empty-handed.

Slowly, slowly, I drag myself up to my feet and start to walk. Every step feels heavy. I thought wearing the gun on my back was the heaviest weight I've ever felt in my life, but no, it's gotta be this. Walking with nothing feels ten times heavier than walking with something.

I'm so in my head that I don't notice the car pulling up next to me until it honks, loud, making me jump.

The passenger window rolls down.

I'm certain then that God must hate me. Because of course, it's Sarah staring back at me from inside the car.

"Get in," she says. In that moment, she sounds a lot like Umma when she's mad. Voice tight. No nonsense. You have no choice but to listen to her.

"How did you find me?" I ask. LA is huge. Sarah might be smart, but she's not psychic. There's no way she would know exactly where to find me.

"Mike said you were trying to get to our store, remember?" she says. "Once I remembered that, I figured you'd have to head down Wilton to Arlington, so I drove this way and kept an eye out for you."

Oh. Right.

"And please don't run away in a stranger's truck again," she says in a warning voice. "I don't know how many more almost–heart attacks I can handle. Seriously, have you never heard of stranger danger? What if that person was a creep?"

She doesn't have to worry about me running away this time. All the fight has gone out of me. Besides, I know she's right. It could have ended up real bad if Luis wasn't a good guy. I had no way of knowing. I get into the car, deflated.

After everything I've been through tonight, it's really

going to end with me going home with Sarah. Umma will probably kill both of us when she realizes we've been out all night. No way we'll both be able to sneak back in without her noticing. A part of me is weirdly relieved. At least I can put off seeing Appa and telling him about the missing gun.

But Sarah doesn't drive us home. Instead, she puts the car in park and turns off the engine. She does a check out the windows to make sure the coast is still clear before turning in her seat to look at me. I expect she's going to let me have it. And then she bursts into tears.

"Why are you crying?" I ask, stunned.

"These are angry tears. Do you have any idea how worried I was about you?" she says, her voice thick. She rummages around the glove compartment and pulls out a Kleenex, blowing her nose. "What happened to your face? Where's Mike?"

I look at myself in the car's side mirror and wince. There's dried blood around my nose and a dark bruise starting to spread around my left eye.

"We got in a fight," I say. "Me and Mike."

"You what?" Now it's her turn to look stunned.

"Honestly, Jordan, what's gotten into you tonight? You're out of control!"

I sigh. "I know. I feel out of control."

I expect Sarah to jump into a lecture. She even opens her mouth to start yelling, but she must see something in my face that makes her pause. For as long as I can remember, Sarah has always known the right thing to do, the right thing to say. But right now, she looks as lost as I feel. Eyes puffy, face red. No words.

"I'm sorry I made you worry," I say, my voice small. "And that I made you angry-cry."

She takes a deep shaky breath, resting her head on the steering wheel. "You have no idea how scared I was thinking about what might have happened to you out here. And when I finally found you, I just got so mad that you wouldn't come with me. That you wouldn't listen." She exhales slowly, blowing a wisp of hair out of her face before lifting her head to look at me. "I know you want me to leave you alone. But I'm your older sister. It's my job to watch over you. That's what Umma and Appa taught me ever since you were born. If something ever happened to you, I don't know how I would live with myself."

There's something in the way she says it that makes me feel like I'm in kindergarten again, when she would sit me down at the kitchen table with the box of crayons and I would ask when Umma and Appa were coming home. "Soon," she'd say. "But don't worry. I'm here to watch over you until they're back."

I know you're just trying to take care of me, I want to say now, *but I don't need you to. I can take care of myself.*

But the words die in my throat because they feel like just another lie.

I look at myself in the mirror again. Bloody nose, bruised eye, no gun.

Maybe I can't take care of myself after all.

"I got suspended from school," I hear myself saying.

Sarah blinks at me, shocked. "What? You did?"

"Everyone knows I'm not as smart as you. I started cheating on tests so I could pull up my grades and show Appa that I could do better. But I got caught. And then I got caught again. And again."

"I don't get it," she says, shaking her head. "Why didn't you ask me for help? I would have helped you."

"Yeah. But I didn't want your help. I wanted to do it

on my own." I look at the dashboard of Sarah's car, where she's got a bunch of Happy Meal toys lined up. They're part of the Potato Head series, her favorite. She loves collecting those Happy Meal toys, always has. But even now, I remember how she used to give me her toys when I said I wanted them because as much as she loved collecting them, she loved me more.

I stare at those potatoes and, maybe it's because I have nothing left to lose, I decide right then and there to confess the rest. "I took Appa's gun tonight and tried to bring it to him. I thought he would need the protection after what I saw on the news. I thought I could be the one to help him. I thought I could prove myself. But then I lost it. I left it in the gardening truck."

I let out a laugh. I guess it is kind of funny, in a terrible way. And then I think of Mike and stop.

"I also punched Mike. And left him in a parking lot. His ankle's sprained."

"Okay, hold on." Sarah holds up a hand. Her face is frozen pale like all the blood's drained out of it. "Can we rewind? Did you say you had a *gun* on you this whole time?"

Um. Maybe it wasn't such a good idea to confess everything.

"Yes?"

She stares at me. And then she slaps me on the shoulder, hitting me with each word. "What. Were. You. Thinking?!" she shouts.

"I told you what I was thinking!" I say, holding up my arms in defense. "How I thought I could prove myself and—"

She raps me on the head with her knuckles. "Ow!" I say. "What was that for?"

"For being ridiculous!" she cries. "Oh my God, Jordan, I can't believe you've been running around the city with a *gun*. And that you hit Mike!"

"It wasn't loaded! Does that make it any better?"

She just stares at me. "Honestly, I don't know whether to yell at you or start angry-crying again."

"I just thought . . . I don't know. I thought the gun would be the only thing to make things better with Appa after our Big Fight. You've seen how it's been lately, right?"

At this, she goes quiet. "Yeah. I have."

"I'm not like you. I don't always know what the right thing to do is."

She chews her lip. "Well, actually, there's been something I've been meaning to tell you." Now she's the one staring at the Potato Heads, looking like she's getting ready to make a confession. "But first, I guess I should tell you that . . . Wow. This is hard."

"Whatever it is, it can't be any worse than everything I just told you," I say.

She's silent for a couple of seconds and then she blurts out, "I'm secretly dating Hae Dang."

I blink. And then I look at her, turning my head so fast I get whiplash. "Wait, *what?*"

"Umma and Appa don't know," she says. "You know they're not his biggest fans."

Whoa. I feel like I can't process this fast enough. Sarah dating? Sarah dating Hae Dang? Sarah dating Hae Dang and keeping it a secret from our parents? I didn't know Sarah had any secrets. Before now, I wouldn't have been able to imagine her ever doing anything that Umma and Appa might not like.

"When? How?" I say. It's not just that I can't imagine

Sarah dating someone. I can't imagine Sarah dating *Hae Dang*. I honestly can't think of two more different people.

"It's been almost a year now," she says. "It started during this one youth retreat. We never really talked a lot before then, but we were on the same volleyball team during games, and Jordan, we dominated. We just played so well together and after that, we started talking more and we found out that we really clicked. After the retreat, we met up a few times to play volleyball together after school and then we just kind of started dating from there."

"So all those times you were coming home late from school clubs?"

"Sometimes I was. But most of the time, I was with him."

She's got this googly look in her eyes and her cheeks are turning pink. "You're blushing," I say.

"I am not."

"You are." I make a face and then add, "I won't tell Umma and Appa."

"Thanks." She smiles. "But there's a second thing I need to tell you."

Now she looks nervous. "That day when Appa found you graffitiing the church, Hae Dang and I also snuck out of service together. We were outside when you and Mike came out. You didn't see us, but I saw you and I was thinking about calling your name, but Hae Dang said to just leave you be. And then a little while later, Appa came out for a cigarette and he saw me and Hae Dang together."

She takes a deep breath. "He asked us what we were doing out there together and I just—I freaked out. I said we saw you and Mike sneaking out, so we came out to look for you. He asked which way you went and I told him. I swear, I didn't think he would get as mad as he did. I didn't even think at all. I just said it and I've regretted it so much ever since. I'm really sorry, Jordan."

I stare at her. All this time, I thought it was just the worst timing ever that Appa came out for a smoke break right where me and Mike were graffitiing the walls. But it wasn't a coincidence? Sarah sent him to us? To try to cover up her own secret?

Somewhere in me, I feel anger start to rise up, but at the same time, it feels kind of weak. Like I've exhausted all my being-angry energy in my fight with Mike and now I have nothing left.

And it's not just that. A part of me is weirdly relieved to

hear that even Sarah can make mistakes. Big ones. She's not as perfect as I thought.

"Jordan?" she says. "Please say something. I'm sorry. I know I'm the worst sister ever."

"You owe me big-time," I say.

"I know I do." She hesitates. "Are you mad at me? I can't tell."

"Yeah. I am. But at the same time, I like you more now than I did before. Is that weird?"

She smiles a bit at that. "Kind of weird. But I'll take it." Then her smile fades. "Listen, Jordan. What you said earlier about how everyone knows you're not as smart as me. You don't have to believe anyone who says that. Even if it's Umma and Appa saying it. A lot of people will expect you to be something in the exact way that they picture it, but it's okay if it looks different for you. Just because you're not me doesn't mean you're not smart or that you're a bad kid."

I'm quiet. I don't really know what to do with that, but the words *bad kid* stick out to me like a neon sign, and I realize it's one of the things Appa said to me during the Big Fight. *I don't understand when you became such a bad kid.*

The thing is, I'm starting to think that maybe it's all a big lie. Good kid, bad kid. Nobody's just one thing. Not Sarah, who's good at school and keeps secrets from our parents. Not Mike, who graffitis the church walls and stuck by me the whole night, even though his ankle was sprained and I kept on making him run.

Not me, who got suspended from school and is trying to make things right with Appa.

"I just want to be the one to decide who I am," I say. I've never said that before, never even really thought it, but saying it out loud now, it feels true.

"Me too," Sarah says.

We sit like that for a bit. "What now?" she says. And I get that she's saying we can choose together, that after everything we talked about, she won't just drag me home.

But I'm not sure. Is it better to go home? Or to go to our store and tell Appa what I did? Before choosing either of those options, though, I know in my gut there's one thing I need to do, and fast.

I buckle my seat belt and say, "Let's go get Mike."

CHAPTER FOURTEEN

Mike's not in the BBQ parking lot anymore. To be honest, I guess I wasn't expecting him to be. He wouldn't just sit around after I left him here. But I'm still disappointed.

"Do you know where he might have gone?" Sarah asks.

I think, hard. He wouldn't go back to Oliver's. Maybe he would try to hitchhike home, but I can't be sure. And then I remember.

"He says he knows a hyung at Silver Star Karaoke," I say. "The spot where we were going to meet Hae Dang." *Your boyfriend*, I add quietly in my head. I'm still not over that. "Hey, does Mike know that you two are dating?"

"If Mike knew, do you think he could keep it a secret?"

"No."

"Exactly." She shakes her head. "You think he might have gone back to Silver Star?"

"Maybe."

"Do you want to go see?"

It might only be a small chance that he's there, but I can't think of anywhere else he would go. We have to try. I nod. "Yeah."

Sarah and I don't talk much while she drives, but it's not bad silence. More like comfortable silence, which I haven't felt with Sarah in a long time. I can tell she's still worried about me by the way she keeps glancing over at my face, probably dying to wipe the dried blood from my nose. Or maybe she's just worried about being outside right now. We've got the news on the radio on, but I don't hear anything new. Every few minutes, I turn in my seat, looking over my shoulder, but I don't see anything like what I've seen on TV. We're still safe, for now.

Sitting still for so long makes me realize how much my body hurts all over. I touch my bruised eye and wince. I'm going to need to roll a hard-boiled egg over it later.

If I'm feeling this bad sitting in a car, how's Mike feeling walking around on a sprained ankle? I feel guilt crawling over my skin for leaving him behind.

I'm the biggest jerk in the world.

We pull up to Silver Star Karaoke and I'm relieved to see that it's still open. I try to peer through the window, but it's tinted so you can't see in. Sarah and I walk through the front door, a bell jingling above us.

"Eseo oseyeo," the person behind the counter says, not looking up. He looks a little older than Sarah, maybe in his twenties, with a pimply face and large round glasses. The noraebang is dimly lit with a disco ball flashing neon lights across the lobby. Down the hall from one of the private singing rooms, I can hear someone belting out a song in Korean.

I approach the counter. "Hi. Are you Brian?"

The guy looks up. He raises an eyebrow in surprise. He probably wasn't expecting a kid to walk in here so late. "Who's asking?" he says.

"I'm Jordan Park. A friend of Mike Rhee. He said he knows you."

He raises his other eyebrow so they're both up in the air now, curious. "Oh. Sure, I know Mike. His parents are friends with my parents."

"Is he here?" I ask.

"No. Why would he be here?"

Disappointment rushes through me. "Oh. I just thought . . . Never mind."

Sarah looks between me and Brian before settling on Brian. "I'm Sarah Park, Jordan's older sister," she says. "Could we wait inside with you for a little bit? We think Mike might show up here eventually. He might still be on his way."

I straighten up. That's right. Mike is walking on a bad foot. It could just be taking him a while to get here.

"I mean, I don't usually let people loiter . . ." Brian looks from Sarah to me. His eyes linger on my bruises and he sighs, taking pity on me. "But it's a slow night. We only have one guy singing here. Just don't bother me."

"You won't even notice us," Sarah says.

He gestures for us to join him behind the counter, where there's an extra chair and a stool. Now that we're settled in, I take in more of the details around me. The first thing I notice is the sound. Tinny Korean voices, speaking through static. I recognize it instantly even though it's turned down low. He's got Radio Korea on.

The second thing I notice is the smell. My eyes zero in on the half-eaten plastic bowl of cup ramyeon sitting on the counter.

My stomach growls.

Dinner with Umma and Harabeoji feels like a million years ago. Brian picks up the wooden chopsticks laid carefully across the bowl. Sarah and I sit and watch him raise the spicy noodles to his lips. I can't look away.

"Um..." He clears his throat awkwardly. "Do you want some?"

He nods to the shelf below the counter, where there are several boxes of cup ramyeon stacked up on top of each other, wedged in between a bunch of microphones and tambourines.

Sarah and I glance at each other. I mean, if he's offering, right?

Five minutes later, Brian is pouring water into our cup ramyeon bowls from the electric kettle in the corner of the counter. We lay our wooden chopsticks across the lids and wait for the noodles to cook. I watch the time. It's already almost ten PM.

"Our phone lines have been ringing all night with stories of the riots in South Central," the man on the radio is saying. His voice is calm but somber. "As always, we are here for you, twenty-four hours a day. For the families whose stores were looted, whose shops were burned down, we are here for you. Please keep phoning in and we will continue to do our best to offer you support. For those in other neighborhoods, particularly Koreatown, be careful tonight. Pay attention. Go home if you haven't already. Remember, there's nothing more important than protecting your own life."

Particularly Koreatown. It sounds like more people are worried about Korean businesses getting targeted, just like Umma and her friend.

"Twenty-four hours a day," Sarah says in awe. "They never stop."

"They keep Koreans in the loop, for sure," Brian says. "People are always calling them when they need help getting directions to somewhere or finding a restaurant's phone number."

"They help with stuff like that?" I say. I lift the lid of my ramyeon and peek inside even though I know it's not ready yet. It just smells so good.

"I know. Funny, right?" Brian says.

For a second, I wonder if they would be able to help me find the gardening truck again. But what would I ask? *Hi, could you help me figure out where this truck went? I don't have the license plate number. And I only know the driver's first name—some guy named Luis. The truck was full of fertilizer and had an upside-down wheelbarrow in the back, though.*

For some reason, I doubt even they would be able to help me out.

Sarah and I dig into our ramyeon. I've had these instant noodles loads of times before, but this is the best ramyeon I've ever had. We slurp as quietly as we can, trying to keep our promise to Brian to be invisible while he works on something on his desk. It looks like he's drawing in some kind of sketchbook. It looks almost like graffiti art, but with a pencil.

"What are you drawing?" I can't help asking.

He moves his arm to cover the paper. "Nothing."

"Oh." I look at the corner of his drawing in the sketchbook, sticking out from under his elbow, and a sudden thought hits me. The day Mike and I wrote graffiti on the church walls, Mike said he got the can of spray paint off a hyung he knows. Based off the style of the drawing, could that hyung be Brian?

If it is, I wonder if he willingly gave a can of spray paint to Mike or if Mike swiped one when he wasn't looking. Or maybe Brian tossed out the can since it was nearly empty, and Mike saved it to write his own graffiti. He did say he always wanted to try.

"So," I say, all casual-like. "Do you see Mike a lot? I'm, um, just curious. He doesn't talk much about his friends, but I think he's mentioned you once or twice."

"He probably doesn't talk about his friends 'cause he doesn't have many," Brian says, not taking his eyes off the page. He flips his pencil around to erase something. "Not that the two of us are friends," he adds. "I just see him at Oliver's now and then, and sometimes he'll follow me around after I leave. Annoying kid. Always talking my ear off. Big imagination, though, I'll give him that."

Huh. I think about what Brian just said, about how Mike probably doesn't have many friends. *Annoying kid*, he said. I remember the way the other kids at church call Mike annoying too. They get swept up in his plans now and then, like the UFO rooftop situation, but other than me and sometimes Ben, I don't see or hear about him hanging out with anyone very much. And what was that thing he said about Hae Dang earlier tonight? *We don't have heart-to-hearts like you and Sarah.*

I mean, I didn't think we did, but I guess the past hour just proved me wrong.

"What kind of stuff does Mike talk to you about?" I ask.

Brian looks up from his sketchbook, annoyed. "Listen, I'm just trying to do my own thing here. I don't really have time for all these questions."

"Why are you doing this here?" Sarah asks curiously. "Why don't you go home? I mean, that's what the radio says."

Brian lets out a slow exhale through his nose. He's probably regretting letting us behind the counter and feeding us ramyeon right about now. "I'm not closing until I have to. Besides, my parents haven't said I should. And I like the background noise when I draw."

At that moment, the lone noraebang singer starts singing extra loud, the sound of a tambourine shaking the walls.

"'Nan Arayo' by Seo Taiji and Boys," Brian says. "Everyone loves that song these days." He turns back to his sketchbook. "Anyway, I'm being careful. I'm keeping the radio on for updates so I can get out of here as soon as I need to. I know what's been going on tonight."

Just as he brings his pencil back to the page, there's a loud *knock knock knock* against the door. He swears, dropping the pencil and dragging his hands down his face.

"Why knock? The sign says we're open," he grumbles, irritated.

Right away, I'm out of my chair, setting the half-eaten cup of ramyeon down on the counter. I run to the door, pushing it open.

And there's Mike, standing on the other side, palms pressed against the window glass, trying to see inside just like I did when I first got here.

Relief floods through my whole body. It's the good kind of drowning. The kind that makes me say *Thank you, God. Miracles are real.*

Mike doesn't look so happy to see me, though. First, he looks shocked. And then he turns around and starts walking away.

"Wait!" I run after him. "Mike, hold on!"

Mike turns around. His upper lip is split and there are bruises on his cheeks where I hit him. We look like a real mess, the two of us.

There's so much to say, I don't even know where to start. I take a deep breath.

"I'm sorry I left you in the parking lot."

Mike folds his arms across his chest. His face is still cold, but he's listening.

"And I'm sorry for the fight. And for blaming you for everything that happened tonight. It wasn't your fault I left my backpack in the truck. That was all me. And ... and ..." I take a breath. "Do you remember that Sunday we graffitied the walls?"

He nods, cautious. "Yeah. Your dad caught us. I felt bad about that."

"Right. And he made us apologize to the senior pastor and we had to repaint the walls."

"Yeah. They were all so mad. Hae Dang was mad too when I told him. Kept saying what a bad choice the name WIZZ was, like no one would have figured it out or something." He frowns. "I thought it was pretty good."

I laugh a little, my voice tight. "I also have to tell you... my dad told me to stop hanging out with you after all that happened. I don't know if you noticed, but I started keeping my distance."

"I noticed."

"You did?"

"Yeah. I did. But I still wanted to be friends."

I look down at my shoes and then back up at Mike. "I'm sorry I did that. And I'm sorry for calling you a troublemaker."

He shrugs. "I am one."

"You're also the best friend I have," I say.

At this, he drops his arms. "Okay," he says. "Fine."

"Fine? We're good?"

A smile spreads across his face. "Yeah. Only because I have no idea where I was going to go just now if you didn't come out and stop me. You know how long it took me to walk here?"

I smile back. "Good."

Mike walks up to me—more limping now than walking, I notice guiltily—and gives me a hug. It catches me off guard, but I hug him too, awkwardly patting him on the back.

"I'm sorry too," he says. "For hitting you. And calling you selfish."

"You put up a pretty good fight for someone with a sprained ankle," I say.

He steps back and examines my face, taking in the blood and the bruises. Then he grins wide, crocodile teeth and all. "I did, didn't I? You look awful."

"Come on," I say. "We're eating ramyeon. After that, Sarah and I can take you home."

"What about your store?" Mike asks.

The relief from reuniting with Mike fades a bit and my smile falters. "I don't have the gun anymore, remember? I'm just going to go back home with Sarah."

I decided that while eating the ramyeon. If I didn't have the gun, there was no point in going to our store. Appa would only worry more that I was there. I could wait to disappoint him when we were both at home.

"There might be a way to get it back," Mike says. He smirks. "I thought of a plan."

Something like hope lifts in my chest.

I should have known.

Mike always has a plan.

CHAPTER FIFTEEN

We're back on the street where we first met Luis. Me, Mike, and Sarah. It's not at all where I thought I'd end up when I first left the apartment tonight with Appa's gun in my backpack. But here we are, about to put Mike's plan into action.

"Here's what I'm thinking," he says. "Sometimes gardeners in my neighborhood will leave their business card in the mailboxes. So maybe—"

"—Luis left a business card somewhere around here since he was picking up something from a client," I finish, putting the pieces together. "Mike. That's actually pretty smart."

"Aren't my plans always smart?" Mike says, puffing his chest out.

I glance at his ankle and then at Sarah, who just shakes her head.

"Right, let's just not answer that, then," Mike says.

Sarah looks up and down the sidewalk, nervous. She was willing to drive us here, but she had the radio on in the car the whole time, listening for updates on the riots. It sounds like things on the looting end might be quieting down but the fires are still raging. "Let's hurry," she says. "It's still not safe for us to be out, especially so late."

"Should we split up and start checking houses?" I ask.

"Yeah. Be stealthy, though," Mike says. "Just remember Hae Dang's three rules. Don't waste time. Don't get hurt."

"Don't attract attention," Sarah says.

"Exactly." Mike nods and then does a double take. "Wait, how'd you know that?"

Her face flushes. "Hey, rule number one, remember? Don't waste time. Let's go."

We split up and start checking houses down the street. I keep my fingers crossed that no one will look out their window and call the cops on us. Not that I'm even sure the cops would come. From all the reports we've been hearing about tonight, they've been really absent. I open mailbox after mailbox, peeking inside, and I can't help but think about that one officer we ran into earlier tonight. I remember what Mike said afterward, about how if you're Asian, people think you're good and quiet and expect you to stay out of the way. To know your place.

I laugh. Whoever actually thinks that's true, I wish they could see us now.

I close another empty mailbox, looking across the street at Mike and Sarah. Sarah is crouching as she checks for business cards, trying to stay out of view of the windows, and Mike is opening and reopening the same mailbox three times, triple-checking as if a card will appear like a magic trick.

It hits me how freaky it would be to be out here in the middle of the night by myself. I'm glad I'm not alone.

We keep looking.

After a while, I feel like we've gone up and down the whole block with nothing to show for it. My hope fades. It was a good plan. Definitely one of Mike's better ones.

But now it's really time to quit.

I drag my feet back toward the others, passing by the houses I already checked, glaring at them like it's their fault for emptying their mailboxes already. And then, out of the corner of my eye, something catches my attention. A flash of white, tied to a doorknob.

I hesitate and then slowly, quietly, make my way up to the door. All the lights are off inside. I expect someone to jump out at any moment and kick me off their property, but no one does. I make it to the doorknob.

There, tied on with a rubber band, is a white business card with the words LUIS'S GARDENING.

And below that, a phone number.

>>>>

"Come on, come on, come on, we have to find a pay phone!" I say.

We scramble into Sarah's car and start driving down the streets, looking for a pay phone. Mike is so excited that his plan worked that he keeps shouting, "I'm a genius! A genius!"

There are pay phones everywhere, but for some reason, it's like when you most need to find one, you can't. I'm just about to get frustrated when Sarah lets out a shout and pulls over sharply, nearly sending me flying against my seat belt.

"Sorry, sorry," she says. "But look! Over there!"

She points out the window. It's dark outside, but I can imagine the angels singing as a ray of light comes down from heaven, beaming a spotlight onto the pay phone on the corner of Olympic and Kingsley.

We all get out of the car and race for the phone, Mike hobbling a few steps behind us. I grab the receiver, business card ready to go in my hand. And then I pause.

"Wait. Does anyone have any quarters?"

Sarah pats her pockets, pulling out an old Hello Kitty coin purse she's had since we were in Korea. "Sorry. I'm empty."

"I have lots of big bills," Mike offers.

I feel like maybe I had some change at the bottom of my backpack, but of course, I don't have that with me right now. I groan, the dial tone ringing in my ear. So. Close.

"Wait! I forgot to check the ashtray!" Sarah says, running back toward the Hyundai.

Mike and I watch, practically holding our breath as she digs through the car, searching. A few seconds later, she lets out a shout of triumph. She jumps back out of the car, nearly knocking over the Potato Heads on the dashboard, racing back toward us with her fist in the air.

"I got it!" she cries.

She holds out her hand, revealing a palm full of coins. Mike cheers and I let out a huge sigh of relief.

"You ready?" she asks.

I nod. "Ready."

Sarah slides a quarter into the pay phone, and I carefully dial Luis's number, my heart pounding. The phone rings.

On the third ring, a woman answers in Spanish.

I tense up. "Uh…Hola." What now? I think of the Spanish textbook sitting in my backpack on the floor of Luis's truck. Load of good that will do me now. I try my luck with English. "Is, um, Mr. Luis there? The gardener?" Or wait. He said he was picking up one of his workers' wallets earlier, didn't he? "Or he might be the business owner," I add.

Luckily, the woman seems to understand. "Wait one moment please," she says. There's a shuffling sound as she pulls the phone away from her mouth. As she calls for Luis, I cross my fingers tight against my knee. *Please, please let this be our guy.*

A familiar man's voice comes from the phone. "Hello?"

"Hi. Is this Mr. Luis, the gardening business owner?"

"Um, yes, it is. Who is this? How can I help you?"

I'm almost positive he's the one, but I won't let myself feel too sure just yet.

"I'm Jordan, one of the kids you gave a ride to earlier tonight," I say.

There's silence on the other end and for a sinking moment, I think maybe I've made a big mistake and it's not the right gardener at all. But then he says, "One of the kids who jumped out of my truck in the middle of the road, yes?"

For the second time tonight, relief fills my whole body. *He's the one*, I mouth to Sarah and Mike. Mike whoops and Sarah grins, giving me a big thumbs-up.

My relief is short-lived this time, though, because Luis does not sound happy to hear from me. Not mad, exactly. But confused. Definitely confused. And more than a little suspicious.

"It's kind of a long story," I say. "First off, I'm sorry for jumping out of your truck. That was probably not what you were expecting at all. The truth is, we weren't going home. We wanted to get to my family's store in South Central but getting there got really complicated. And I ended up leaving my backpack in your truck. It's really, really important to me, that backpack. I was wondering if I could come and get it?"

There's a low murmuring sound as he speaks to someone in Spanish and I realize he's probably doing exactly what I'm doing with Sarah and Mike and recounting the whole conversation to the woman next to him, maybe his wife. "It's the weird kids from the truck," I imagine him saying. "The ones that jumped at a red. Literally jumped."

Finally, he clears his throat. "I will check if your backpack is in the truck," he says. "Here's my address. Do you have a pen?"

"Um . . . just a second," I say. *Pen, pen*, I mouth to Sarah, making a writing motion with my hand.

Her eyes widen. She makes a mad dash back to the car, digging around again for a couple of seconds before running back with a pen in her hand. Seriously, thank God for that car and for my sister. She's always prepared.

"Ready," I say to Luis.

I recite the address to Sarah as Luis speaks it over the phone to me and she writes it on the back of her hand.

"Thank you so much," I say. "And again, I'm really sorry. About everything."

I mean it too. I've been running away from a lot of people tonight. Sarah. Mike. Luis. All people who were trying to help me in their own way.

Luis grunts. "See you soon, then." And he hangs up the phone.

>>>>

The drive to Luis's house is quiet, mostly. But my thoughts feel loud. All night I've been thinking about bringing the gun to Appa and what I'll say to him when I do. I thought it would prove to him that I can be the person he wants me to be. Someone who can do things right for a change.

But now I'm not sure what I want to say to him.

"This is it," Sarah says.

She slows down in front of a house and I immediately

see the gardening truck in the driveway. The wheelbar-row's gone, but it's definitely the one.

"We'll be right here," she says.

Mike gives me a thumbs-up from the back seat, where he's sitting with his leg stretched out. He's done walking for the day. Honestly, he probably would have been done a long time ago if it wasn't for me. I give him a thumbs-up back and get out of the car.

I feel weirdly nervous walking up to the front door. I wipe my sweaty hands on my jeans, ring the doorbell, take a step back. A sudden thought hits me. *What if Luis looked inside my backpack?*

But it's too late to do anything about it. The door swings open and he's standing there, changed out of his painter's pants and into a gray sweatsuit, holding my JanSport in one hand and the hand of a sleepy-looking little girl in the other. She has pigtails and is wearing a big orange T-shirt with a sun wearing sunglasses on it.

"Hey, kid," he says.

"Hi, Mr. Luis." I turn to the girl. "Hi..."

"Natasha," he says. "My daughter. She woke up from her sleep and won't leave my side."

"Sorry," I say, feeling bad. "Was it the doorbell?"

"Bad dream," he says. Natasha blinks at me and yawns. He hands me my backpack and lifts her up into his arms. I guess he didn't look inside my bag after all because he passes it over, no questions asked.

I take my backpack. I thought I would feel that same flood of relief again, finally getting it back. But instead, it feels strange, holding a gun in my arms while Luis is holding his daughter in his on the other side of the door. It doesn't feel right to have it near her.

"I hope you're not getting into too much trouble tonight," Luis says. His eyes linger on my bruises.

I don't really know how to answer that so I nod instead, hoping that's enough.

"Good night, kid."

"Good night, Mr. Luis. And happy birthday, Natasha."

He closes the door, Natasha waving a little hand at me. After the door closes, I don't move for a second. Then I slowly open my backpack, checking inside.

There's the gun case. And the Spanish textbook. And my Walkman. All right where I left it.

Now it's time to go finish what I started.

CHAPTER SIXTEEN

The windows of the liquor store are boarded up when we get there.

It's a place I've seen so many times before. But tonight, it looks different. I guess I've never been here so late at night. It's nearly eleven PM now. And I've never been here with a gun either. The gun kind of changes everything. Makes the air around me feel heavier somehow. Sarah, Mike, and I sit in the car for a while, just staring at the store.

"If the windows are boarded up, that means Appa was here," I say.

"He wasn't home when I left," Sarah says. "So he might still be."

We sit there, staring.

"So are we going in?" Mike asks.

He and Sarah both look at me. This whole night started with my decision. Now they're waiting for me to take the final step. They're ready to go with me, Sarah and Mike. But I think this part, I need to do alone. I'm still not sure what I'm going to say to Appa, but whatever it is, I know it needs to be between the two of us.

"I think I need to do this part by myself," I say.

Sarah starts to object. "We can't just leave you here. We don't even know if Appa's inside."

"If he is...," I say, "if he is inside, then I need to talk to him by myself."

The car is quiet again.

"Well, then," Mike says. "What are we waiting for?"

We get out of the car and go right up to the door and start knocking. We bang our hands against it, knuckles bruising, and when no one comes, we start yelling.

"Appa!" Sarah and I yell. "Appa!"

"Jordan's dad!" Mike yells.

Just when I think maybe he's not here anymore, Appa's face pokes out over the roof of the store. I can hear his gasp all the way from where I'm standing on the ground. "Sarah? Jordan?"

"And Mike," Mike says.

Appa's face disappears. I picture him coming down from the roof, walking fast through the aisles, opening the door. And then he's there in front of us. Shocked. The shadows under his eyes darker than I've ever seen them.

"Annyeonghaseyo," Mike says, remembering to greet his elder properly. He bows his head.

"What are you doing here?" Appa says.

For a moment, we just stare at him, and I think both me and Sarah must be thinking the same thing. *He's okay.* After spending the whole night trying to get to him, I almost can't believe he's really right here standing in front of us.

"I have something for you," I say.

Sarah puts an arm around Mike's shoulder. "We're just dropping Jordan off," she says. She looks relieved and a little misty-eyed, seeing Appa, knowing that she's leaving me with him. "I'm going to take Mike home now."

I look at her gratefully. I guess I really don't give Sarah as much credit as she deserves.

She's not so bad.

"Does your mother know you're here?" Appa asks, still bewildered. "And what happened to your faces?" He looks at me and Mike.

"I'll explain everything," I say.

"We'll be okay, Appa," Sarah says. Before she turns to leave, she puts her arms around Appa and buries her face in his chest, hugging him tight, eyes squeezed shut.

I've never seen Appa so thrown before, like he doesn't know what to do at all. Even as he pats Sarah on the back, a whole battle passes across his face like a storm cloud. I can almost see the questions he's fighting. Does he let Sarah go? Make her stay? What about Mike? What's with his ankle?

"We'll be okay," Sarah says again, pulling away. She smiles now and walks backward toward the car, waving. "See you at home."

Appa and I stand at the door of the liquor store as they get into the car. Mike rolls down the window.

"Jordan!" he calls. "Next time we hang out, it'll be at Ben's for Nintendo. For real. And I'll get us burgers—my treat."

He grins. I grin back.

Then he rolls up the window and they drive away.

Leaving me and Appa alone, just the two of us.

We go up to the roof.

"The phone line's been down," Appa says as we make our way up. "That's why I haven't been able to call. It took me a long time to get the boards from Home Depot. It was really busy there and the traffic was ridiculous. I only just finished boarding it up a little while ago."

"Why were you sitting up here?" I ask. We take a seat on upside-down plastic crates, red and blue. Cigarette butts litter the roof at my feet and I can tell he's been up here for a long time. I wonder if it was just to smoke and keep watch. "Why didn't you come home right away?"

He doesn't answer that one. Instead, he puts his hands in his pockets, leans forward on his crate, and says, "I think it's time you tell me what *you're* doing here."

This is it. My moment.

I zip my backpack open and pull out the gun, holding the case out to Appa.

"I came to bring you this," I say.

He stares at it.

Then he stares at me.

"Where did you get this?" he asks. He takes the gun case and his face grows angry. "Jordan? Answer me. Is this the gun I told you never to touch?"

I swallow hard, rushing to explain. "Yes. I took it from your closet when I saw the news. I knew you were out here and you didn't have any protection and I didn't want you to get in trouble. What if you had nothing to defend yourself with? I mean, it's not loaded or anything, but I thought just having it with you could make a difference. I thought...I thought I could help you."

It's not exactly how I imagined saying everything to Appa, but I'm so nervous, my words come out all tangled. I look down at my feet, digging my palms into the crate, leaving little X marks all over my skin. "I thought I could help you," I say again, quieter now.

At first, I think Appa's going to start yelling, but instead he looks up at the smoky sky, takes a deep breath, one, then two, like he's trying real hard to stay calm. Then he looks down at the gun case in his lap. He slowly opens the case and—there it is—the pistol, cradled inside like a jewel. He looks at it only for a couple of seconds before closing the case again, clasping it shut.

"Jordan," he says, and I think, *This must be the night of first times*. The first time I heard Sarah swear. The first time I punched someone in the face and got punched in the face. The first time I hear Appa say my name in this voice, kind of complicated and sad and angry and gentle all at once.

"I didn't forget to bring the gun with me," he says. He says each word slowly like he's scared he'll lose control of them if he goes too fast. "I left it behind on purpose. I didn't bring it because I never, ever want to have to use it on anybody."

I blink, trying to understand. "But . . . for protection—"

"It's not protection," Appa says. His voice goes firm now. "It's a weapon."

He sighs, running his hand down his face. We're quiet for a long time and when he starts speaking again, he's looking right at me, his eyes on mine.

"Back when I was in Korea, there was a time when I was a courier for the air force. It was during the Vietnam War. I always had a pistol on me when I was on duty because I was carrying official documents. Like all men in Korea, I learned how to use it during my time in the military."

Appa's never shared anything about the air force before.

He's like Harabeoji in that way. He hardly shares anything about his past. I grip the edge of the crate, listening.

"One time during a run, I was at a restaurant and a man came in. Drunk. Loud. He was yelling at the people in the restaurant, making a scene. I tried to take him outside, but he kept at it, and he started getting violent. Hitting people, throwing his drinking glass, spitting. It was ugly. I managed to drag him outside, but then he pulled out a knife and charged at me, so I took out my gun." His eyes get kind of glassy then, like he's back there, seeing it. "He started taunting me, waving that knife in my face, saying go ahead and shoot me, I bet you don't have the guts. He got to me more than he should have and . . . I took a shot. I aimed right by his ear and pulled the trigger.

"I'll never forget the way he screamed. I shot past him at the wall, but if I'd aimed a little to the left, I could have killed him. It would have been so easy. It should never be that easy to hold someone else's life in your hands. People have no idea what they're doing when they pull the trigger. I did it to scare him because in that moment, I was feeling mad. But could you imagine if, in that split second, I decided to actually shoot him? If the trade-off for my moment of anger was the cost of someone's life?"

I look down at the gun on the roof, imagining Appa holding it in someone's face and pulling the trigger. It's hard to picture, but it must be true from everything he's said. "Why do we have one, then, if it's such a bad thing?"

He looks out to the streets now, somber. "Jordan, your dad has made a lot of mistakes. I brought us here to America because I thought we could have a better life, but it hasn't been easy. I've failed us more times than I can count." He lays his hand down on the gun case, palm flat. "I got the gun because I felt like the rules were different here. The police couldn't protect us if anything bad happened, and it was my job to do everything I could for our family. A job I was already not so great at doing. But then when I heard what happened to Latasha Harlins, I realized things aren't so different here after all. People will make a lot of terrible choices in the name of protection. I was reminded of what I already knew."

Protection. This whole time, that's how I was thinking of the gun. As a shield. But a gun isn't a shield. A gun is a gun. It's meant to kill people.

I think of Latasha Harlins and my whole stomach sinks. To her, the gun wasn't protection. It was the opposite. It was death.

"I'm sorry, Appa," I say, hanging my head. "I shouldn't have brought it. I just wanted to do something to help you and show you that I'm not a total failure."

He turns to look at me again, his face full of open surprise now. "A total failure? What do you mean?"

"I . . . got suspended from school today," I say. "I've been cheating on tests so I can get better grades." I fold my hands together and unfold them, trying to find the right words. The ones that will help me say what I really want to say. "I'm sorry. I didn't mean it when I said any family would be better than you. And I didn't mean to blame you for what happened with the last store. It's just, you're always disappointed in me, and there's all this pressure not to let you down. I thought the cheating could make things better, and the gun too, but I feel like I just always make everything worse. I'm just never enough."

Appa gets sadder and sadder the more I talk, and I think I've made the biggest mistake of all time. Telling the truth.

But then he reaches over and puts a hand on my shoulder.

"I've said a lot of things lately that I shouldn't have said. And I haven't said a lot of things that I should have said."

"Like what?" I ask quietly.

"You are not my biggest disappointment. I regretted it as soon as I said it. And of course we wouldn't be happier if we just had Sarah. Our family wouldn't be our family without you." He winces. "I know I've said some rough things lately. I'm sorry. I haven't been thinking straight. My mind feels all over the place."

I think of Umma and Appa's hushed conversations, Umma saying *Don't worry don't worry*. "Is it because of money?"

He pauses like he's trying to decide how honest to be. "It is," he says. "But it's also this whole place. America." He gestures out with his arms toward South Central. "Like I said, we came here to give you a better life. But are we really doing that? You seem to be struggling so much. I worry that I made a mistake for you. And then I see the news, I see things like what's happening today with Rodney King and the riots, and I think, wow. I brought my kids here. I thought I could give them everything. But what is really here for me to give?

"If I'm hard on you, it's because it comes from this place where I still want to believe we made a good choice. That you can still have a better life here if we fight for it. I'm sorry that it doesn't come out that way sometimes. I never learned how to be a good dad."

A good dad. I never realized Appa thought about whether he was a good dad or a bad dad the way I think about being a good kid or a bad kid. I remember my conversation with Sarah in the car, how maybe stuff like this is never so simple, and that goes for our parents too.

I nod because I don't have any words for how it feels to have the weight lifted from my shoulders, to feel like I'm not buried under a rockslide anymore.

He nods back. He gets it, and I realize it's not just the store that looks different tonight. Appa looks different too. It's weird. I don't really know what it is. Maybe it's that Appa has always just been that—my dad. But tonight, he also looks like his own person. Regrets and all.

I wasn't sure exactly what I was going to say to him until I got here. But now that I've said it, now that I've heard what he has to say back, I realize I've finally gotten it right. Not by cheating or by proving myself. But by saying the truth.

It seems way too simple. To say sorry when you're sorry. To say you're hurt when you're hurt. To say something's not right when it's not right. But it's one of the hardest things in the world. And today, I did it.

I just want to be the one to decide who I am, I said to Sarah. I'm not always sure who that is yet. But I think it might be someone like this.

I hear voices from down on the street. It was empty but it's slowly starting to fill up with more and more people, and I'm not sure if they're part of the riots or the protests or something else completely.

"What should we do now?" I ask.

"Now, I think, is a good time to go home," he says.

He puts the gun back in my backpack and zips it up, carrying it in one hand. He puts his other hand around my shoulders and we go down from the roof, back into the store. Together.

EPILOGUE

May 8, 1992

It's been just over one week since April 29, the day some Koreans have started calling Sa-I-Gu. Four-Two-Nine. The day that changed everything.

The LA riots went on for five days. On April 30, day two, Koreatown was targeted. I watched on TV as Korean men went up to their store rooftops to protect their shops, guns in hand, military training kicking in. Or maybe it was just survival instinct. The police didn't help. I don't think many of us expected them to.

From the riots, sixty-three people died, over two thousand were injured, and more than one thousand buildings were damaged or completely destroyed. Looking back now,

I can't believe I was out there on that first night. I think about how bad things could have gotten if I was in the wrong place at the wrong time. I was lucky. Umma's reminded me of that at least a hundred times since that night.

When I got home with Appa from the store, she was on me before I even had time to take off my shoes, slapping me hard on the back. "Do you"—*smack*—"have any idea"—*smack*— "how worried I was?" She had tears in her eyes, and Umma hardly ever cries. I said sorry. A lot. And then I sat at the kitchen table with her and Appa and Harabeoji and told them everything, Sarah sitting right next to me to share her part.

Since then, I've watched a lot of TV. Mostly because I was suspended from school, but also because I became Harabeoji's personal servant as punishment for everything I did. You know. The cheating, the suspension, the sneaking out with Appa's gun, the hitchhiking with a stranger . . . all of that.

To be honest, Umma and Appa didn't really know what to do with me after I told them the whole story. They were everything at once—relieved I was alive, shocked that I did so many wild things in one night, mad that I had made them worry so much. But they didn't know what the right punishment would be. So for now, they've passed me off to Harabeoji. I refill his ojingeo plate. Flip the pages of his book when he's reading. Massage his feet. Do basically whatever he asks me to do whenever he asks me to do it.

I know that's not the end of my punishment. It's barely even the start. But I have a feeling it'll take us a lot longer to figure it all out, to learn how to even talk about what happened that night. It's a lot. But the wall between me and Appa has finally lowered and it's easy to breathe around him again. And for that at least, I'm real glad.

I'm about to help Harabeoji cut his toenails when the phone rings. Perfect timing. "I'll get it!" I jump up to answer it before Harabeoji can call me back. "Hello?" I say, picking up the receiver.

"What's up, dude?"

It's Mike. I grin. When I told Umma and Appa about everything that happened on the night I went out, I made sure to say I couldn't have gotten through it without Mike. Even with all the fighting we did, that's the truth. Appa may still not be Mike's biggest fan, but he's okay with us hanging out together again. As long as there's an adult nearby.

"Hey," I say. "How's Oliver's?"

"Please don't say that name to me," Mike groans. "I'm so tired of it here."

When Sarah dropped off Mike that night, his parents were waiting for him. They put the pieces together and figured out that he was the one in Oliver's when his dad showed up with the gun. The restaurant key in Mike's pocket proved it. They made him return all the money, take shifts at the restaurant cleaning every corner until it sparkled, and sit on his knees every night for ten minutes with his arms in the air.

"I'll take the kneeling punishment over cleaning the grease trap any day," Mike says. "How are you doing with your grandpa? You got off so easy."

I think of Harabeoji's toenails waiting for me, and I grimace. "We're doing okay. But remember, I told you, this is just the beginning. My parents have been busy helping their friends who lost stores in the fires, but I'm sure they're still thinking of the best way to deal with me. They told me so themselves."

Maybe it was because Appa boarded up our shop early, but our liquor store was spared from the fires. Though, to be honest, I don't know how much the boards would have helped if someone had decided to light the place up in flames. Like Umma said, we got lucky. But a lot of other families didn't.

Over two thousand Korean-owned stores were either looted, damaged, or totally destroyed in the riots. Throughout the past week, people would phone into Radio Korea with calls for help—food supplies, legal assistance, all sorts of stuff—and Koreans across the city would answer, gathering in church parking lots with food donations, volunteers coming together to help rebuild what was lost. Even President Bush came to visit Koreatown and specifically Radio Korea to show his support. Umma and Appa and their friends have been talking about that nonstop. It was a big deal.

"For the longest time, I just felt like a Korean person living in America," Appa told me the other night. "But now, rebuilding together, I think this is the beginning of feeling like I am Korean American."

I've thought about that a lot since he said it. How the riots felt like the end of a lot of things, but as terrible as they were and as much as I hope they'll never happen again, it was somehow also the beginning. Maybe for the whole city.

"Anyway," Mike says on the phone. "I called to tell you that I overheard Hae Dang talking on the phone with Sarah the other day. Sarah, as in your sister Sarah! Since when were they friends? Weird, right?"

I stifle a laugh. "Huh, yeah. Weird."

I've still kept Sarah's secret like I said I would. She said she's just waiting for the right time to tell Umma and Appa. Meanwhile, she's started tutoring me in school. I don't think I'll ever be up to her level in Mr. Martins's eyes, but she said she never liked him anyway.

Mike and I talk for a bit longer and then hang up. When I go back to the living room, Harabeoji's asleep in his chair with the TV on. *Yes!* I'm spared from the toenail clipping, at least for now. I pick up the remote to turn the TV off and pause, staring at the news on the screen.

It's a recap of the events leading up to the riots. As I watch Rodney King, the Latasha Harlins murder, and the acquittal of the four police officers, it hurts in a new way. Then it shows Koreatown. Or at least, what used to be Koreatown. I stare at the burned-down buildings and the rubble, remembering the men on the rooftops with their guns, trying to protect their stores. And this hurts too, seeing how Koreans were targeted, knowing the police did nothing about it.

That's another thing I've thought about a lot, ever since

Sa-I-Gu. How protecting yourself and the people you love is complicated, especially when the people who are supposed to protect you don't. It's tough, just like figuring out how to change a whole history of injustice, like Mr. Gary shared.

That night I came back from the store with Appa, Umma kept shaking her head and saying, "Why would you do this? Why?" But Harabeoji, who was sitting silently at the table the whole time, just said one thing: "We need to protect what's ours." He understood why I did what I did.

And now I think, yeah, we do. But I also think of Mr. Gary, who helped patch up Mike's ankle, Luis who gave us a ride, Brian who made us cup ramyeon and let us wait in his noraebang. Maybe we need to protect what's ours. But we also need to protect each other. Maybe that's the real kind of protection.

My dad named me Jordan, after the river. I never thought I could live up to that name. The expectation of peace and freedom on the other side. The chance to be better.

I still don't know if I'll ever really be able to live up to it, but here's the thing about rivers. They never stop running. Toward the ocean, toward something bigger than themselves.

Maybe in that way, we're all a bit like rivers.

AUTHOR'S NOTE

This wasn't the book I was supposed to write.

It was supposed to be a middle-grade mystery novel—a gift to a younger me. Middle grade because those were the years when I needed a place of my own, worlds that didn't intersect with my family or school. Mystery because it provided a place where the nonsensical made sense, at an age when I was learning that the world didn't always operate as promised. And what validation it would have been to see a face that resembled mine on the cover of such a book!

As the year began, I was looking forward to what I thought would be a fun detour from my day job. But 2020 conspired against fun.

The pandemic began killing us and drove the rest of us indoors. George Floyd's murder broke our hearts. The protesters who risked their lives to demand justice in his name uplifted us. A wave of anti-Asian violence prompted many of us to call our parents, asking them to curb their daily walks, to carry mace and pepper spray.

My wife and I struggled with how much to expose our children to, and how to talk to them about it—not that we were able to process it with much clarity ourselves. Day after day, sequestered in our house (or more accurately, our kitchen), washing produce and trying to come up with something new for dinner, we had little else to do but think and reflect.

I began to think about another incident of police brutality that occurred when I was eighteen years old. On March 3, 1991, a Black man named Rodney King, while being arrested for speeding and evading arrest, was beaten within an inch of his life by LAPD officers.

And I thought of something that happened only a couple of weeks after that: Latasha Harlins, a fifteen-year-old Black girl, was murdered by a Korean American shop owner, Du Soon Ja, who thought Harlins was stealing a bottle of orange juice.

Du served no time. And on April 29, 1992, a jury acquitted the officers who beat King. In response to the verdict,

Los Angeles burned. And perhaps in response to Du's light sentence, Korean businesses burned.

The similarities to George Floyd, or more specifically, the lack of progress between then and now, was stark and damning.

I started to measure the progress of other things. My father encouraged me and my brother to watch TV as children to learn English, in the hopes that language would make us accepted as Americans. Did he continue to harbor that hope as he saw those fires burning, fourteen years after he and my mother brought us to America? And did I believe we had been accepted since, almost thirty years later? And our children—were they going to ask the same questions?

Over the years, I had toyed with the idea of telling a story about the LA Riots from a Korean American perspective. But the path forward never seemed obvious to me. More honestly, since I was imagining a film, I didn't see a part for myself, so I never put much energy into the idea.

But now, maybe because I was thinking so much about how to discuss the events of 2020 with my children, I began to think about what the events of 1992 must have been like for a kid.

And so the idea started to come together: a boy who wants to deliver a gun to his father for protection on a night when the whole city shook with anger.

Immediately, I struggled with whether a gun should be a part of the story, whether it would be irresponsible. And while I was hesitant to write a story for children about a child with a gun, I did think it was unfortunately realistic.

I recalled a childhood Korean American friend of mine, whose father owned a gun. One day after school, he and a friend were playing with it, unaware that it was loaded. It went off. The hole in the wall behind him revealed the bullet had sailed dangerously close to his ear.

I thought of my first time shooting a gun. My eighth-grade Sunday school teachers, a wonderful young married couple recently transplanted from Arkansas, had invited me to spend the night at their home. They cooked me dinner, treated me to a movie, and in the morning, took me to a shooting range.

I imagine they must have seen an awkward kid who needed a rite of passage. As a child, I had played with toy guns; now they were going to teach me respect for the real thing. They showed me how to load and shoot a pistol, then a rifle; indeed, I gained a lifelong respect for the power of guns. I have never since associated them with those childhood feelings of fun and play.

Finally, I thought of my children, seven and twelve, who had already gone through active shooter drills at their respective schools. I concluded that it was naive of me to think that I could shield any kids from the reality of guns in America. Tragically, they were already living it.

Race was another topic that gave me pause—how should I present these ideas to a young audience? Again, I thought of my children. They had been watching the news. They knew what the protesters were marching for. They knew that people were attacking Asians. They saw that someone had spray-painted the word "China" below the word "Stop" on the sign at the end of our street. It just didn't seem like a time to be polite anymore. In fact, sanitizing the truth too much struck me as a disservice, an abdication of our responsibility to prepare them for independence.

Whatever attitudes about race that our story uncovered for Jordan, whether it was coming from outside his community or from within, we decided to leave in if it felt authentic.

In fact, my cowriter, Sarah Suk, and I operated on a loose rule of thumb: Anytime we had an opportunity to connect details in the story to details in our lives or to people we knew, we did so. As a result, even though I didn't know anyone directly whose businesses were burned, writing became an unexpected excavation of very personal memories.

But wait. As I said, this wasn't the book I was supposed to write. After hatching the idea, I hemmed and hawed— did I really want to do this? Eventually, I summoned the courage to email my editor, Alvina Ling, with a dim pitch for an entirely new book. I was sweating it—I mean, I was essentially asking for permission to break our agreement. And the only thing I could offer her in the way of justification was "I don't see myself being able to stop thinking about all this stuff for a long time," which was and remains true.

To her unending credit and my unending gratitude, she said yes.

So we were off. And it was only toward the end of the

project that I recalled another time I was waiting for someone important to me to say yes. Coincidentally, it must have been around the time of the riots that I told my father that I intended to major in English, a dubious path to financial freedom (of course, he didn't know then that I would have another doozy for him a few years later, when I would tell him I intended to try my hand at acting). He considered, and said, "Okay. Well, maybe you can write a history of Koreans in America." A qualified yes, but a yes nonetheless.

I guess he was trying to make himself feel better. Translated: "If you're not going to make money, maybe you can at least contribute something to your community." I was nineteen, so I resented what I interpreted as a burden on a young man starting his life.

But as we finished the book, I recalled this moment, and thought I had more in common with Jordan than I thought. Maybe this book, a work of fiction and not the history he offhandedly suggested, was indeed an offering from a troublemaker son to his father. Not history, but maybe it could at least be insight.

Though we settled on the title, *Troublemaker*, late in the process (not without some trepidation on my part, as we were invoking the titan John Lewis's admonition to get in "good trouble"), I did find the writing from the beginning to be an exercise in examining what is good and bad trouble. I thought about who gets to decide who's a troublemaker, and who gets to decide what trouble is. I hope you and my father read the book as intended: the good kind.

—John Cho

ACKNOWLEDGMENTS

Firstly, my thanks to Sarah Suk for the structure she gave to a jumble of ideas and reassuring an anxious first-timer.

To my wife, who always disagrees with me when I tell her I can't do something.

To my children, my ace-in-the-hole authenticity readers.

To my representatives—Troy Zien, Jo Yao, Chris Hart, Albert Lee, and Alex Kohner—without whom I wouldn't have dared imagine something this audacious.

To Alvina Ling and Ruqayyah Daud for saying yes to the more difficult path.

To Charlene Allen, D. Ann Williams, and Christine Suh for their indispensable early feedback.

To Johng Ho Song for his service at Koreatown Youth and Community Center and pointing me in the right direction.

To Richard Choi for his service at Radio Korea, and to

his family, for their first-person account of those harrowing days.

To Chef Edward Lee and Scott Jo for their late 80s/early 90s memories.

And to Scott Chiplin for keeping it all together on my behalf.

—John

First and foremost, thank you to John. Somehow through the magic of technology, we were able to pull this book together from opposite ends of the world. We did it! Collaborating with you has been the coolest. Thank you for trusting me to be on your team.

My deepest gratitude to Alvina and Ruqayyah, without whom this book would not be what it is today. Thank you also to Albert, Mr. and Mrs. Choi, Jen Harris, Charlene Allen, D. Ann Williams, and Christine Yi Suh for all your wisdom and guidance.

As always, all my thanks to my agent, Linda. From beginning to end, your support has been everything.

Lastly, thank you to my family and friends, my joy and my rock. Special thanks to Sue O for being by my side, every step of the way, every word on the page.

—Sarah